THE
LAST FRAME

THE
LAST FRAME
JIM WRIGHT

Carroll & Graf Publishers, Inc.
New York

Copyright © 1990 by Jim Wright
All rights reserved

First Carroll & Graf edition 1990

Carroll & Graf Publishers, Inc.
260 Fifth Avenue
New York, NY 10001

Library of Congress Cataloging-in-Publication Data

Wright, Jim, 1950–
    The last frame / Jim Wright.—1st Carroll & Graf ed.
      p.   cm.
    ISBN 0-88184-569-8 : $16.95
    I. Title
PS3573.R53665L3   1990
813'.54—dc20   90-1657
                                                CIP

Manufactured in the United States of America

For my daughter someday

All characters and incidents in this book are pure invention. They have no existence outside the imagination of the author and are not related to or based on any persons bearing the same or similar names, or to any actual events.

Grateful acknowledgment is made to Lillybilly Music for permission to reprint lyrics from "Slow Turning" by John Hiatt. Copyright 1988 by Lillybilly Music. All rights reserved.

FOREWORD

The Last Frame was written in memory of Arthur Fellig (1899–1968). Fellig, better known as Weegee, is still regarded as the world's greatest crime photographer.

Armed with a Speed Graphic and a police radio in his car, he roamed New York City during the 1930s in search of fresh corpses and soured dreams. Weegee's exploits provided the inspiration for this novel.

Prologue

Ten feet above the walkway, a lone figure hung silhouetted against the night. One arm clenched the four-inch-thick braid of steel cable. The other arm steadied a rifle butt.

The bridge trembled under the swell of rush-hour traffic, and the figure struggled to keep aim on his target: a young white man grappling with two policemen fifteen yards down the railing.

"Come on, turn this way, give me a shot," the figure muttered. "I can't hang on much longer."

Then, as if on cue, the teenager squirmed free. The man clutching the tightwire squeezed off three quick shots. And stopped the kid dead in his tracks.

Chapter One

THURSDAY NIGHT

The man propped against a pay phone in the shadows of the George Washington Bridge was about to negotiate a kill fee.

As he dialed, he ran a quick inventory: temples pounding, shoulders stiff, hands raw, feet numb. All he wanted was a warm bar and a cold beer.

For an instant, he began to think his pal Bingo was right. Chasing life's losers with a loaded Canon was a job fit solely for the hard of thinking. Photographers who worked Italian weddings in Astoria made twice the money, and contending with the mother of the bride was a Roman holiday compared to his latest tour of duty.

Moments earlier, he'd straddled a support cable on the George Washington Bridge, bucking a thirty-mile-an-hour head wind and sub-freezing November temperatures to shoot some hysterical teenager who probably had no intention of jumping to a conclusion anyway. After all of the hassles he had overcome—navigating the outbound crunch of motorists on Riverside Drive, abandoning his car in mid-span, shinning up a cable to get a decent angle—the kid went limp when he saw Carver's camera and offered feeble resistance when the Port Authority cops finally collared him on the walkway.

No guts, no glory. Fainthearted jumpers were hardly news in a city with dozens of bridges and thousands of losers, and he was certain the *Daily News* was going to cut its losses and pay him a token fee rather than run the picture. Hell, the money wouldn't cover the cost of the custom-made rifle stock that had steadied the barrel of his two-hundred-millimeter lens.

Now he found himself at a public phone in Fort Lee, New Jersey, coaxing his fingers back to life and trying to make the one call that might salvage his day.

In Alphabet City that morning, he'd taken some shots with Page One potential. Some coked-out pimp was strolling down Avenue B with a .38 planted in a hooker's jaw, and he had arrived in time to catch the dude pull the trigger. . . .

"Ralph? This is Will Carver. Sorry about the noise, but I'm in Jersey. I got some shots of the jumper for you. Nothing major, unfortunately. The cops grabbed him before he could take the plunge."

Ralph Dempsey, Carver's contact at the *News*, told him the inevitable—to forget about the jumper. And when Carver asked about the kill fee, Ralph coughed and said he might find a spot to run the photo, then changed the subject. An hour earlier, someone had called the newsroom in search of Carver. Free-lance job, the man had said.

Carver didn't pay much attention. He cared more about the roll of Plus-X he'd delivered that morning. "Just pay me fifty bucks for the jumper and we'll call it even. I'm more interested in the pimp shot. Still talking Page One?"

The reply didn't please Carver, and he shuffled his feet more out of agitation than to get the circulation in his toes going again. The pavement around the booth was strewn with spent cigarettes. "Well, I guess it's your decision. . . . Yeah, you got it. . . . Talk to you tomorrow."

That topped off the day: Ralph had said the editors at the news meeting wanted to go Page One with a shot of Madonna barging through a crowded nightclub. Didn't those college-bred geeks know by now that sensationalism sells more papers than celebrities? Movie stars go out on the town every night to get their pictures in the tabloids, but how often does a drug-drenched pimp blast one of his employees in public? Not more than once a month.

Ralph Dempsey's remark stuck in Carver's craw: "We're trying to upgrade our image." It didn't matter that his pictures might be Pulitzer material if a guy from the *Times* had taken them. In the *News*, they'd always be splatter shots.

And he'd always be ol' Carver, ambulance chaser. He bristled at the thought. So what if his cigars were relit and his preferred headgear was a faded Phillies cap? So what if he favored an old peacoat and jeans to a Banana Republic jacket and pleated slacks? So what if he hung around the emergency ward at Bellevue, waiting for botched suicides and accident victims? So what if he spent half his nights in the Ninth Precinct station house? If rapists and gangsters got booked at three A.M., you couldn't photograph them by phone. Maybe some editors at the *News* considered him low tide, but they had to admit nobody took pictures like his. Nobody came close.

No use in getting steamed. It was late. He was beat. He still had to drive back to Greenwich Village, and the West Side Highway had its quota of maniacs any hour of the night.

As he walked to the driver's side of his 'seventy-eight Rabbit, he breathed deep and tasted winter, crisp and cold on his throat. He cursed to himself when he noticed the dents in the trunk again—some addict must have pried it open that morning in Alphabet City. He shivered. The job, the city were closing in. He had turned forty today, not that anyone noticed, and the incident with the jumper only underscored what he already knew. His camera bag felt heavier and heavier of late, and the night chill lingered longer in his bones. Free-lance crime photography had always been right up his alley. Now it had become a dead end.

He huddled in the Rabbit a few minutes, watching his breath steam the windshield while he waited for the heater to kick on. He'd get the trunk fixed tomorrow. It locked, but it'd be too easy to jimmy. Right there went a hundred dollars. In car insurance, as in divorce, no-fault was another way of saying he'd foot the bill.

Chapter Two

Once his feet had warmed enough to work the pedals, Will Carver threw the Rabbit into gear and felt it shudder to a halt. As usual. He turned the ignition key again. The engine sputtered, and the oil light on the dashboard flashed red. He checked the odometer. Two hundred miles had gone by since he'd added a quart of oil. He was too cold to add another. It could wait a day. He wanted to get home.

It wasn't that he had anything personal against the mainland—it was just that the thought of being anywhere east of Shea Stadium or west of the Hudson made him fidget. The suburbs were too safe, too normal. For a photographer who trafficked in calamities, suburbs were graveyards with two-car garages.

The Rabbit kicked over on the third attempt to restart it, and he proceeded to navigate the snarl of roadway leading to the George Washington Bridge. He paid his toll in crumpled dollar bills, then eased into the Manhattan-bound traffic.

When he'd crossed the bridge, he relaxed. He was on home turf again. He thought about his phone conversation with Ralph Dempsey at the *News* and the prospects of a free-lance assignment. Maybe it was a corporate job. As much as he detested shooting product shots for annual reports or corporate honchos for some house organ, the right assignment could mean a down payment on a less-used car.

The daydreaming cost him. As he merged onto the West Side Highway, a black Jeep Cherokee zipped past and veered into Carver's lane, nearly clipping a fender. The driver waved his right arm, pointing to the narrow shoulder as if he wanted Carver to pull over. But Carver wasn't about to stop for some stranger, not at night, not on a barren stretch of the West Side Highway.

Carver flashed his high beams to proclaim his annoyance, then accelerated into the middle lane. The Cherokee cut in front again, still trying to get him to stop on the shoulder. Carver clicked his high beams. This time he left them on.

The Cherokee retreated to the slower lane. When Carver went to pass, however, the Cherokee swerved left. Carver had to downshift and push the four-banger to the wall to get by.

Who was this guy? Some run-of-the-mill hothead, no doubt— pissed at the world and venting it in Carver's direction.

Carver weighed his options and ruled out help from the police at once. In fifteen years on the West Side Highway and the FDR Drive, he'd never seen a blue-and-white. No, his best chance was to stay cool and avoid confrontations: You never knew when the other guy might be crazier than you.

Carver attached his seat belt, then looked in the side-view mirror for the Cherokee. For a minute or two he thought the vendetta had passed. The Jeep lay back twenty yards or so. To his right, beyond the guardrail, the Hudson River roiled with whitecaps.

Where was traffic when you needed it? The only other southbound car was a battered blue Valiant. It was plastered with religious stickers—obviously the sort of vehicle to avoid on the open road.

Just when he'd forgotten the Cherokee, he sensed headlights hurtling toward his rear bumper. He braced for the impact. Even though he'd buckled his seat belt, the jolt thrust him into the steering column and sent the Rabbit careening out of control. It scraped the guardrail, then lurched into the middle lane.

Carver mashed the gas pedal to pull out of the skid. A hundred yards later, the Cherokee approached ramming speed again. At the last instant, Carver swerved right and managed to catch the Ninety-sixth Street exit.

The Cherokee stayed on the West Side Highway. No matter. Carver hadn't planned on stopping to exchange driver's licenses. This guy was a sicko, even by Manhattan standards.

Carver drove south on Riverside Drive. His mistake. Seventy-ninth Street was the next exit off the West Side Highway, and the Cherokee was waiting.

Carver held one unspoken advantage: The Cherokee was new, and his white Rabbit had seen several years of duty in Lower Manhattan. He couldn't get any new dents. He could only rearrange old ones.

Thus, when the Cherokee pulled alongside at Seventy-sixth Street, Carver made his move. He jerked the wheel to the left and sent the Cherokee skidding across the faded double line.

The Cherokee slid in front of a stopped bus and slammed over the curb. A jogger dived for cover. Somehow, the Cherokee pulled out of its tailspin and went charging down the sidewalk, still in the hunt.

At Seventy-second Street, Carver ran a red light, turned right, and curled onto the West Side Highway northbound. The Cherokee followed. One hope remained: Harlem. If he could stay ahead of the renegade Cherokee long enough, he'd reach the no-man's-land of meat-packing plants and deserted warehouses.

He had a destination in mind—an alley where he once photographed a stiff from a drug deal gone sour. The alley ran between two worn-out brick slaughterhouses. The owner had planted a steel I beam in the pavement to keep young hoods from stripping cars there and abandoning the carcasses. If Carver's calculations were on target, the Rabbit could slide through the gap. He wasn't so certain about the Cherokee.

Ahead, an old Buick freighter chugged along in the right lane, fifty yards from the exit. The Cherokee loomed ten yards behind. Carver shifted into third and watched the tach hit the red line as the Rabbit sailed past the Buick in time to catch the exit ramp.

For a moment, Carver figured he was safe. No luck. As he reached the end of the ramp, a pair of headlights flared in the rearview mirror. Carver gunned the engine. The dashboard rattled as the Rabbit raced down a washerboard street to the factories.

When the alley came into view, Carver downshifted so the Cherokee could close the gap, then he cut the wheel hard and closed his eyes. Tires squealed. A fender scraped the wall.

An instant later came the thunderclap of metal meeting brick.

* * *

THE LAST FRAME

When he'd caught his breath, Carver unhooked his seat belt and reached for his camera bag. He grabbed a loaded Canon with a fifty-millimeter lens already attached.

By the time Carver climbed out of the Rabbit's passenger side, the Jeep's driver was screaming for help. The area reeked of gasoline.

Carver circled the Cherokee and tugged open the driver's door. Blood had spattered the windshield and now trickled from the man's mouth as he spoke: "Help . . . me."

"You run me off the road, and now you want my help?"

"Carver. Please."

It took an instant for the words to sink in: The guy knew him by name. He had been set up. This guy wasn't some stray bullet—he'd been aiming for Carver all along.

Carver grabbed the man's collar: "Tell me who you're after, and I'll get help."

The man coughed blood. "Queens," he said slowly, and gasped for breath.

Carver shook him by the lapels: "What?"

"Ace—" Carver couldn't catch the rest of the words.

The man's face turned ashen, and death dribbled from the corner of his mouth. Wouldn't you know it, Carver thought, the guy died about as well as he drove.

When Carver let go, the man collapsed against the steering wheel. Carver retreated ten feet and adjusted the camera settings. Times such as these were why he used a Canon instead of a Nikon, the standard news photographer's camera. Nikons were tough to focus in low light, and if you made your living by taking pictures of human cockroaches, you probably preferred a Canon or an Olympus.

After he shot five frames, Carver let the camera hang by its shoulder strap and wondered if any of the pictures packed the wallop needed to make Page One. He considered setting fire to the Cherokee and shooting the flames, but he'd already been accused of doing that more than once, and the fire department had enough problems with Harlem firebugs without risking their necks trying to pull a stiff from a burning Jeep.

No, he needed to find a hook that would set this apart from the countless other car wrecks he had photographed over the course of two decades. He stepped back five paces and saw the faded sign painted on the brick wall a few feet above the smashed Cherokee.

Carver looked through the camera and inched forward until he had a perfectly framed shot: the head slumped over the steering wheel, the blood-spattered windshield, and the sign that proclaimed: FRESH MEAT.

He finished the roll of Tri-X, rewound it, then turned and jogged to the Rabbit. He didn't want to be there when the scavengers descended.

When he reached Ninety-sixth Street, he found a pay phone and dialed nine-eleven, on the off chance the guy in the Cherokee still had a pulse. Then he drove to the *News*. It was ten P.M. With luck, his new photo would make part of the press run. He wouldn't get paid as much, but he'd sleep more soundly, knowing he'd knocked Madonna off the front page.

An hour later, he unlocked the door to his walk-up on MacDougal Street to find the place ransacked.

Chapter Three

There's a story about one of the original *Daily News* photographers. The story's in a book, so it must be true.

It was the early twenties, and the man was the first Inquiring Photographer. Each day he went to a different locale and asked pedestrians a different opinion-provoking question. After a few days, their pictures and replies ran on the editorial page.

One of the first questions he was assigned was "How do you know you're sane?" The photographer dutifully asked a few passersby and got printable answers. But when a fourth man was asked how he knew he was sane, the man became agitated and accused the photographer of persecuting him.

The photographer replied, "What are you, some kind of nut?"

The guy shouted no, and to prove his point, he reached into a pocket and pulled out a release certificate from the local loony bin. Then he punched the photographer in the mouth.

The wreckage in Carver's apartment reminded him of that story: If you were a newspaper photographer in New York City, you never knew when you'd cross paths with a crazy—on the job, on the West Side Highway, or in your own living room.

Strange thing was, Carver's railroad flat hadn't been a palace to begin with. Yet somebody had taken the time to trash it further. Then there was the security system, which Carver heretofore had considered foolproof. Each day before he left his apartment, Carver turned the radio dial to the country music station and cranked up the volume. A normal burglar would've heard Randy Travis crooning and made two fast assumptions: somebody must be home, and he'd be wielding a shotgun at the very least.

Not earlier today. On the floor, two lenses lay battered and a hundred-sheet box of photographic printing paper sat open and exposed. Then Carver saw the sprung rat trap in the middle of the floor and felt better about the world.

As a precaution, he always set a trap inside his padlocked camera bin. The guy who'd trashed his place must have gotten a tad too curious, pried open a corner of the lid, reached inside, and had his fingers mangled for his trouble.

Carver smiled. He'd made his point. Mess with him and you needn't worry about any cops. Retribution would be sure and swift. It was in his Scottish blood. "Nobody attacks me with impunity": the credo of his forefathers' homeland. The intruder, of course, had no way of knowing this until it was too late. Tough.

But what did the intruder want? The lenses were broken, not stolen. Three Canon bodies had gone untouched. His old Speed Graphic, with its Polaroid attachment still loaded with film, sat undisturbed on a tripod in a corner of the kitchen. Then he remembered his precious pictures.

Carver went to the kitchen toilet and lifted the tank's lid. Nothing had been touched: There, taped inside, was an airtight plastic bag with the silver prints for a book of photographs he was compiling. He dubbed them his "Manhattan Project": portraits of hermaphrodites and hookers, derelicts and panhandlers, killers and flashers.

On first glance, they seemed little more than snapshots of Manhattan's dregs, but the best pictures went beyond that. They were images of people who'd dropped their guard, if only for an instant, or had no guard left to drop. The faces showed pain, rage, sorrow, desperation—emotions protected more closely than wallets in Times Square.

A photo of a homeless woman huddled beneath a billboard advertising a Trump casino, a shot of a dead junkie with a syringe still stuck in his forearm, a picture of transvestites trawling the Tenderloin District. He leafed through the black-and-white prints and thought of Weegee, his idol, whose pictures of Manhattan's mean streets had inspired Carver to photograph the city's misbegotten souls.

Alas, as his former wife used to remind him, he had assumed the eccentric old photographer's bad habits as well. They accounted for his ramshackle appearance, rude cigars, and street ethics. They also contributed to the abrupt end of his marriage and, he sensed, his current mess.

He walked to the refrigerator. On the top shelf, a six-pack stood next to a dozen neatly stacked boxes of Tri-X and Plus-X. If it had been junkies or vandals, the beers would've walked. No, this was a professional job, and the culprit had probably jimmied the car trunk as well. The guy in the Cherokee? Maybe. Whoever did it sought something in particular—maybe something in that caché of photographs taped inside the toilet tank.

What if there had been more than one intruder? Carver was too exhausted to worry. He double-bolted the door, then reached into his camera bin and extracted a .22-caliber pistol reserved for scaring the bejeezus out of any Jehovah's Witnesses who came door-to-door. He loaded the pistol, then went to the terrarium by the couch. In the excitement, he'd forgotten his roommate.

He tapped the glass. "Port Authority, you can come out now." No reply. Carver couldn't tell if the hermit crab was dead or if it just refused to answer to its name. Carver had spotted it in a pet store and said, "Cripes, the only place you can get bigger crabs than this is the Port Authority bus terminal."

Carver had liked the line so much he bought the crab—so he could use the joke again when company came to call. Few people stopped in, but Carver became attached to Port Authority anyway—to the point where it was hard to tell who was the bigger hermit and who was the bigger crab.

He tapped the glass again and said good-night. He reached above the kitchen sink and flicked on the amber photo safelight. He had rewired it so the rest of the lights in the apartment would switch off automatically whenever he had to do darkroom work. He then sat on the couch and waited for the intruder to return.

Carver fell asleep at four A.M., the pistol still in his hand. He dreamed of aiming his Canon at a pair of muggers and blowing their brains out.

Chapter Four

FRIDAY MORNING

At ten A.M., Will Carver awoke to the sound of sanitation engineers testing the tensile strength of galvanized aluminum trash cans outside the apartment building. As soon as he fell back to sleep, the phone jangled him awake again. It was Ralph from the *Daily News*.

"Good morning, Carver. I'm working the early shift today and thought I'd call with some good news. We ran your crash photo Page One. The pimp and the jumper ran inside. I put in a voucher for you and signed your name. Still use an X, don't you?"

Carver ignored him.

"Got something else that might interest you," Ralph continued. "I got a call a few minutes ago from the feds asking about your photo of the car wreck—apparently the guy who died was a buddy of theirs. They wanted to know how you happened to be in the bowels of Harlem about the time their pal wrecked his Jeep."

"Just lucky, I guess."

The other end of the line fell silent. Ralph's problem was that he took everything too seriously. He was one of those editors who seemed to be around the newsroom all hours of the day or night and never let up. Ralph had been married once, for three years, and Carver never could decide if Ralph got divorced because he was so consumed by his job or if Ralph was so consumed by his job because he got divorced.

In either case, Ralph didn't see any humor in carnage and, for Carver at least, that was a major flaw. Journalists couldn't afford to cringe about death and destruction—not if they wanted to sell newspapers. And giving readers a ringside seat at a car wreck definitely sold more papers than giving them the lowdown on the governor's latest tax proposal.

Finally, Ralph spoke again. "Come off it, Carver. A man is dead, and the feds want to talk to you about it. I said you usually stopped by around six."

"Fine. In the meantime, do me a couple of favors. First, could you call the morgue and see if the guy in the Jeep had any broken fingers? Don't ask why, just be a pal. And when you get an ID on him, check the clips. Something doesn't jibe."

"Carver, you holding out on me?"

"You gotta promise me a cone of silence, but the guy in the Jeep crashed trying to run me off the road. Answer me this. Why would a fed be after a small-time camera jockey like me? I don't shoot national secrets unless they frequent transvestite bars or Times Square pool halls."

Ralph's voice became animated. "Do I hear you right? You got shots of a senator with a hooker or something? I'll reserve Page One right now."

Typical Ralph. Thug eats a dashboard sandwich, he's uptight. But he gets wind of a politician fooling around with a fifteen-year-old, he's in tabloid heaven.

"You'd be the first to know," Carver answered. "Lord knows I need the bucks. I'm broker than Venus de Milo, and some idiot ransacked my place yesterday. Mangled three hundred dollars' worth of lenses. I'll be on the Bowery trying to get some lenses cheap, and I'll head uptown later.

"One more thing: You said over the phone last night that somebody was looking for me for a free-lance job. Did he say what it was about?"

"No. The guy just asked if you were around. I told him you were out shooting a jumper on the G.W."

The comment woke Carver up: That explained how the guy in the Cherokee had found him. He must have waited for Carver to come off the bridge. No doubt the call from the feds was bogus, too. Somebody was after him, but who—and why?

"Carver, you still there?"

"Sorry, I had my mind on something else. What kind of shots you shopping for today—the usual?"

Ralph hemmed. "Truth is, I'd like you to lay off the mondo bizarro stuff. How about shooting celebrities? That's where the dough is. You see the shot of Liz Taylor and her latest boyfriend in yesterday's *Post*? I hear it cost the *Post* five grand. I'm looking for that kind of stuff, just not at those prices. For instance: A PR man called to say that Priscilla Presley will be at that trendy new nightclub in TriBeCa tonight, and he guaranteed a good headlight shot. Show up at seven-thirty with your camera loaded. No kill fee if she's a no-show. This one's strictly on spec."

Carver balked. "Come on, you know how much I hate those shots. . . . Okay, but make it worth my while. See you around six if you're still there."

After he hung up the phone, Carver opened the venetian blinds to see what kind of day it was. The window provided the usual tired view of the air shaft—laundry on five clotheslines running from fire escape to fire escape. Carver wondered if his neighbors ever took in their wash. It hung there every day, faded as the November sky.

In the kitchen, Carver splashed cold water on his face and put on some water for coffee. While it heated, he gathered a week's worth of empty beer bottles and dropped them into the kitchen trash can. They joined cottage cheese containers, potpie tins, and other bachelor culinary debris. He decided that when he'd saved up enough money he'd buy a microwave and live high off the hog for once.

He checked the thermostat: a balmy seventy-eight degrees. The apartment was above a restaurant kitchen, making it one of the few cheap flats in Manhattan that didn't want for heat after September. By noon each day, in January or July, the temperature in the apartment reached ninety degrees, and the oppressive heat had long ago forced Carver to abandon his plans to use the kitchen as a darkroom.

The kitchen's one nice feature was that it also housed the

shower and the toilet, and a tenant could wash up and cook at the same time—a definite time saver after a long night's work.

The trouble was, a night's work took longer and longer, and his pictures made the *News* less and less. A few years earlier, the paper had been printed in red ink—nearly going bankrupt a few times—and it couldn't justify many free-lance shots after it had forced so many staffers to take early retirement.

As he sipped his instant coffee, Carver tried to sort out the events of the past twenty-four hours again. He didn't like the idea of some creep rummaging through his apartment, and liked even less the idea of being run off the road.

He tried to make sense of the man's final sputterings—about aces and queens, or aces from Queens? Nothing made sense. And what did any of this have to do with a deadbeat photographer like him?

For inspiration, he looked at the hand-stitched sampler over his sofa. The sampler sported a pair of clasped hands and Carver's version of the Lord's prayer: "Forgive Us Our Press Passes."

It reminded him of the time not long enough ago when he broke the rules to get a photo of a maniac who'd abducted a shopgirl, and Carver had nearly gotten the girl blown away in the process. . . .

His mind was wandering as usual, and he didn't have much time to get ready for the afternoon ahead. With his two wide-angle lenses out of commission, Carver would have to stop by Bingo's Pawnshop in the East Village to pick up replacements on credit.

He bent to unlock the camera bin and felt a sharp pain across the base of his spine. A bad back from lugging equipment had ended more press photographers' careers than bad eyes or bad judgment, and Carver's had begun to go. He stayed under the shower an extra ten minutes, then rubbed Ben-Gay on the small of his back.

When he felt he was ready to face Manhattan, Carver threw on a pair of old Levis and reached into the closet for his one white shirt. It was buttoned from the last time he wore it, and a tie still hung from the collar. The tie was deep blue, relatively clean, and within an inch of being in style.

He knew that if he waited long enough, fashion might catch up to him again.

Chapter Five

Will Carver put on his peacoat and left his apartment by the fire escape window. He negotiated the two flights of ladder, then dropped the final ten feet to the pavement. He took the fire exit onto MacDougal Alley, put his collar up to ward off the bitter November wind, and looked to see if anyone was following him. The lane was empty.

Carver fetched his Rabbit from the garage on West Third, added a quart of oil, and drove across town. The motor oil brought immediate results. The Rabbit stalled only once during the trek.

He found a parking space on East Seventh Street near McSorley's. He would've parked a few blocks away in a zone reserved for the press—NYP plates in Manhattan were akin to a Get Out of Jail Free card in Monopoly—but no matter what part of town such zones were in, the spaces always contained the fancy imported cars of media executives who hadn't filed a story since the days when Dan Quayle was knee-high to Howdy Doody.

After pumping a quarter into the meter, Carver reached behind the front seat for the canvas camera bag, leaned under the seat for two Big Mac wrappers, and tossed them onto the passenger seat. On the dashboard he set two take-out coffee cups. For a spell, he'd fallen into the habit of placing a diaper on the dash to discourage thieves, but by summer the smell had become overpowering.

Whenever colleagues at the *News* told Carver he was too paranoid, he had his answer ready: The automobile was invented in Germany in 1889. The radio was invented in Italy in 1895. The car radio was invented in Manhattan in 1911, and it was stolen an hour later. In these parts, car windows were broken more often than politicians' promises.

In his haste yesterday morning, Carver had neglected to trash the Rabbit, and, sure enough, somebody had pried open the trunk on the hatchback just to look around. The culprit hadn't taken anything—not even the darkroom equipment on the backseat. But why take that chance now? The car was parked midway along the muggers' commute to the Village, their main turf for separating tourists from their jewelry, cameras, and pocketbooks.

Bingo's Pawnshop, a couple of blocks away, was a retail outlet for hot merchandise. Two types of wares graced Carver's old buddy's shop—stuff that took ten years to move, and stuff that took ten minutes. Acoustic guitars hadn't sold since Bob Dylan lost his touch and found religion. Guns, gold, and cameras were another matter.

Nothing had changed since Carver's last visit. On a shelf to the left, dust-encrusted toasters resembled miniature tombstones. Below them was Bingo's used-blender collection. Black-and-white TV sets, returned after the World Series a month before, graced the floor.

Carver threaded his way past them to Bingo's counter, housed in inch-thick Plexiglas. It felt like visitors' day at the state pen. Bingo's crime was fencing stolen goods—and murdering the English language.

"Hey, Picket, what's shakin'?"

"Carver, for the thousandth time: I'm tired of your assinuendos. If you keep saying I'm a fence, I must insist you take your patronizing elsewhere."

"Come off it. I'm not just your one and only friend, I'm your best customer. Anybody steal Canon equipment last night?"

"Funny you should ask," Bingo said. "Some swank dresser was in no more than five minutes ago. Sold a complete outfit. Said he needed the money for his daughter's intuition at Swarthymore. I'll sell you the works for three hundred dollars, including the case."

Bingo balanced his cigar butt on the edge of the counter and produced an aluminum Halliburton case. Carver popped the clasps, opened the lid, and extracted a Canon F-1 body. He ran off a few frames at the fastest and slowest shutter speeds, checked the body for dents (a bad one lurked in front of the hotshoe), and inspected the innards.

"Bingo, where'd you get this stuff, Afghanistan? It's been through a war, probably on the Russian side."

"What'd you expect for three hundred dollars, mint?"

"Tell you what," Carver replied. "Keep the Canon body and the case, and lend me a wide-angle for the weekend. I'll give you twenty bucks up front and even clean it for you."

"Okay, but only because I like you," Bingo said. "In fact, you're really getting populated around here."

"Meaning what?"

Bingo knew he had Carver going, and he milked the moment. He relit the stump of his White Owl, smelling up the joint even worse, and tried to change the subject. "How 'bout them Jets?"

"Knock it off, Bingo. Who's looking for me?"

"Well, if you're going to act pissy about it. . . . A couple of suits were here yesterday asking if I bought any Canons lately. I think they were deferring to that F-1 body I sold you on Wednesday—the one that had the free film inside. Of course, I didn't tell 'em nothing."

"Fat chance," Carver said. "How much it cost them to worm my name out of you?"

"Fifty bucks, since you asked. It was like stealing—I mean, I already told 'em you'd be in soon. They said they were in a real hurry to get the camera back, seeing as how the pictures had sedimental value. Said they'd make it worth your while. I told them you worked for the *Daily News* a lot. They didn't find you?"

"I think I must have bumped into one of them last night. And for all I know, the other one's probably waiting for me right now. I'd better leave through the back. Meanwhile, if one of those guys returns, tell him he's got a deal. I'll give him the camera. I'll give him the film, even make up some nice prints for him. What he does with them is his business. I don't need the aggravation. And watch yourself. These guys aren't choirboys."

"And who do you think I am—Mother Teresa?"

Chapter Six

At the corner coffee shop, Will Carver took the far booth and sat facing the street. He needed time to plan his next move, and he didn't need any more surprises.

Carver had spent the better part of his life trying to avoid trouble, but it never did him any good. Like on Wednesday, when he saw the Canon at Bingo's and became intrigued by the notion that it had film inside. How was he to guess, until he developed it, that the roll contained shots of a man and a woman in various stages of overexposure?

The pictures had to be what the stiff in the Cherokee was after. But what did playing cards have to do with it?

Carver scratched his neck, trying to come up with a plausible answer. He must be missing something, he decided, and he probably would find out what it was soon enough. Why did Bingo have to tell those two men his name, or say that he'd be back? The thugs probably were watching Bingo's shop now, and if they didn't see him leave the shop soon they'd go in after him. Thank goodness for back doors.

Carver thought about using the pay phone to call Joe Gold at the station house a couple of blocks east—he might be on duty—but dragging the cops into it went against the grain. If you couldn't take care of yourself in New York, you'd be dead sooner than later anyway.

Carver figured he was safe—at least until he surrendered the pictures. Bingo, on the other hand . . .

Carver walked to the pay phone.

"Hey, Picket, I was just thinking about the two guys who asked about that hot Canon," Carver said when Bingo answered the phone. "I ought to tell you I found a roll of dirty pictures inside the camera body that I bought from you two days ago. Now you're connected to those pictures, and you may be in for trouble. So is the guy who sold you the camera. I've got to warn him. What can you tell me about him?'"

Carver fished a pen out of his peacoat pocket, scribbled "The Puma" in one of the few remaining public phone books in Manhattan, then ripped out the page. "Did you give them this kid's name, too? . . . Where can I find him? . . . One more thing . . . "

Bingo sounded bored. "What's the big deal? I've got my sawed-off shotgun under the counter."

"Bingo, I know you've handled some tough customers in your time, but I'm telling you these guys are big-league. You've got to get out of there as soon as you can, maybe even leave town for a while. And don't come back until you read about it in the papers. It's going to blow over—or blow up—real soon."

Carver returned to his booth, loaded the Canon, and advanced a few frames. He figured if Bingo didn't clear out quick, somebody would be on this roll of film, horizontal.

Even from inside the coffee shop, it sounded like somebody had dropped a safe from twenty stories up. Bingo must have visitors. Carver grabbed the camera, tossed the rest of his gear to the woman behind the counter, and barreled out the door.

He turned north on the Bowery in time to see a man running toward Fourteenth Street. Carver froze, focused the Canon, and fired four quick shots with the motor drive before the man turned the corner and disappeared.

With one hand securing the camera, Carver raced toward Bingo's. The door was standing open. Carver craned his head inside. "Bingo, it's me—Carver. It's safe now."

Silence.

"Bingo?" In the distance, Carver could hear police sirens. He inched toward the counter. Instinct told him it was over, even if the Plexiglas appeared intact and no bullet holes were visible. Then Carver saw the red smear on the plywood paneling behind the counter and followed it down the wall to where Bingo lay.

His cigar had fallen into his lap and was now burning a small hole in his grubby wool slacks. Bingo's right hand still gripped the shotgun.

When the cops arrived, Carver flashed his working press card and explained what had happened to his friend. The cops smashed through the door to the partition, and by the time they bent to check Bingo's pulse, Carver was standing atop the counter and taking pictures.

One cop, a rangy patrolman in his mid-twenties, told Carver to stop, but Carver ignored him. Finally the cop grabbed him by the belt and pulled him off the counter. "What do you think you're doing, camera man? I thought you said you were this guy's pal."

Carver raised the Canon to his right eye again and resumed shooting. "When he was alive, Officer, he was my friend," Carver said between frames. "When he died, he became news."

Chapter Seven

In a run-down walk-up office on West Fourth Street, a bare-chested man with ash-blond hair and an athlete's build moved in for the kill. The man led with three left jabs, *rat-a-tat-tat*, then bobbed, grunted, and landed a perfect right cross. Staying on his toes, he started to circle clockwise, then threw the same combination.

This go-'round, his timing was off. His fist glanced off the thick leather punching bag, causing him to lurch forward. Must be the damned leather-soled Bally loafers, he decided. No way to get the proper footing on the polished oak floor.

When Brud Siracusa had regained his balance, he started to walk away, then abruptly wheeled and landed a hard left that caught the bag flush. Brud clenched his fist in the air and broke into a smile as he walked toward his desk. Nothing lifted his spirits like a well-thrown sucker punch, unless it was a well-thrown sucker punch that connected with jaw instead of leather.

Now, just as he wanted to relax, he could feel the adrenaline kicking in, and he breathed in until his lungs filled with air, then slowly exhaled. After he calmed down, he wiped a towel across his chest. No sense in letting sweat stains ruin a sixty-dollar shirt. He glanced at his watch. Eleven-thirty. Had to look sharp, in charge, when Mo Orsinski returned. And Mo would be back any minute now. With a little luck, he'd have the film, and then they could get down to business.

The white silk shirt fit snug against his tightly muscled back and chest as he buttoned it. He tucked the shirttails into his pleated slacks, picked up a thin black tie, and walked over to the mirror on the wall by the window. He tied the knot carefully and inspected his reflection in the mirror. He cursed under his breath: His little workout had caused the cut on his left cheek to reopen.

Otherwise, Brud Siracusa decided, he was looking pretty good for a man on the wrong end of a ten-thousand-dollar gambling debt. The knife mark had been a reminder that the debt was overdue, and Brud had no choice but to chalk it up to the cost of doing business. Hell, if that moron hadn't shanked the field goal, he'd be on Miami Beach right now.

Brud looked in the mirror again, and smiled. He had a Teddy Kennedy nose—it took a wrong turn at the bridge—but other than that his mother's comment ten years ago still held true. His face was too pretty to waste on a boy. Maybe so, but his lovers never seemed to mind.

He pushed his hair back across the top of his head, and he was reaching into the top desk drawer for his brush when he heard the click and the voice over the intercom: "Brud, it's me. Buzz me up. We got more trouble."

Brud pressed the buzzer that unlocked the main entrance below, then walked to the door of his real estate office. Calm down, he told himself. Nothing you can't handle. He adjusted his tie and wiped a bead of sweat from his brow. Had to look under control at all times, especially in front of a nervous Nelly like Mo.

He opened the door at first rap. A stocky man with a cowhide jacket and shiny brown polyester pants entered.

"What's up?" Brud asked.

"I screwed up bad, Brud. I just killed some guy—the pawnbroker." Mo Orsinski had thinning hair the color of rust and a pitted complexion that grew redder as he spoke.

"The pawnbroker? What's the pawnbroker got to do with this? We weren't going to pay him another visit until this afternoon."

"I followed the photographer, just like you told me—he's a crafty son of a bitch. Tried to sneak out the back door to his apartment house, just like you said. He got in his car and drove straight to that pawnshop we traced the camera to. I figured he must be returning the pictures or something, so after a few minutes I decided I better go in after him. The photographer had vanished, and the pawnbroker must have known what I was after. He was waiting with a sawed-off cannon. I beat him to the trigger. I didn't have a choice.''

Brud ran his fingers through his hair. "Anybody see you?"

"Not really."

"Not really? What's that supposed to mean?"

"I don't think anybody got a good look at me."

"What happened to the photographer?"

Mo winced as he took off a pair of smooth black leather gloves, and Brud could see how swollen the fingers on Mo's right hand were.

Mo unbuttoned his jacket as he answered Brud's question. "He must have gone out the back or something. I know it's not my say-so, but this is turning into a disaster. First I ransack the guy's apartment and almost get my hand snapped off by some frickin' rat trap—"

"You were wearing gloves, Mo."

"It still hurt like hell. Let me finish. I nearly lose three fingers in this guy's stinkin' rat trap, then you send Tony to tail him and Tony ends up dead—with his face on the front page of the *Daily News*, no less. Now I follow the photographer and end up blowin' away some lame old man. All for nothin'."

"Sit down," Brud ordered. "Get a hold of yourself. Sure, Tony screwed up. He was told to talk to the damned photographer, not play bumper cars with him. That was my fault. I never should have brought in an outsider. But you did fine. The pawnbroker could have connected us to the camera. He had to be killed anyway."

Brud looked out the window as he spoke, hoping that Mo wouldn't challenge him on the lie, but Mo was busy taking off his cowboy jacket and placing it on the back of the metal office chair.

Mo wore a white polo shirt that hid neither his barrel chest nor the beginnings of a beer gut, and he was trying to tuck his shirt into his pants when he spoke again. "I'll calm down when I'm good and ready. Crap, you owe me for two jobs already. I got reason to be pissed off."

"Fine, Mo. We've been over this before. We get the pictures back, we work our little deal, and you not only get your money, you get a nice fat bonus. Come on, you're talking to old Bruddy boy here. Now just answer me a couple more questions. What'd you do with the gun?"

"I got it with me." He patted the pockets of his jacket, then retrieved the .38. "See?"

"Fine. You might want to unload it now. Wipe it down good, then when you leave, go to the basement and toss it in the furnace."

"No need. No fingerprints to worry about, Brud. You know I always wear gloves."

"Ever hear of ballistics?"

Mo nodded, removed the bullet clip and slid it back into his coat pocket, along with the gun. "As I was saying, this scam of yours is down the toilet. I say we cut our losses while we can and try blackmailing some other chump. This ain't worth all the grief."

Brud walked behind the desk and stood with his arms folded. He'd once bought an audiotape on management styles, and this was supposed to be a power posture. It had worked every other time he'd tried it, but then the people he'd used it on were illegal aliens in arrears in rent and scared to death of being booted onto the street.

And when tenants didn't get the message, Brud found that his knowledge of boxing proved to be an effective collection tool. He'd tell renters to come up to the office, and if they didn't have the money, he'd amble over to the punching bag, throw a vicious uppercut, then tell them they had twenty-four hours to pay up. They paid up. If they didn't, that's where Mo came in.

Intimidating tenants was the only thing he liked about the landlord business—and the reason he'd gotten the job in the first place. Brud hated nickel and diming dense foreigners who didn't understand English but did understand punching bags. Hated this dump of an office, with its peeling paint on the ceiling and the poorly plastered walls. Hated never making money to get ahead. Hated the past-due notices on two credit cards. Hated the calls from the loan shark.

Brud's cheeks burned at the thought of the loan shark. The guy had come to call yesterday with his flunkie and the straight razor.

At least Brud hadn't trembled, hadn't flinched a bit when the slob guided the blade lightly across Brud's cheek.

Brud stood behind the desk for a few moments while he collected himself. "Mo, trust me," he said. Then he placed his open palms on the desk, another power pose. "We're still in control here. Nobody's going to connect you with the death of that old fart pawnbroker. Put the clamps on a couple of things, we're rich. No more penny-ante scams. You read me?"

"But if we don't got the film, how we gonna blackmail that guy?"

"Like I said, let me worry about it."

"And you're certain he's going to pay big bucks for some lousy photographs?"

"He can't afford not to, my friend. He can't afford not to." Brud's mind raced as he plotted their next move. Yesterday Mo had gotten the pawnbroker to give him the name and address of the kid who'd stolen the camera—in case Brud wanted to get even—and now that information would come in handier than Brud had thought.

"First things first. The kid who stole the camera is named Puma, right? You got a good idea of where he lives. We already know where this guy Carver lives, and we know he works for the *Daily News*. So we're still in business. We'll get that film back soon enough, easy as collecting rent."

"But what if the photographer goes to the cops?"

"With what? If he tells the cops how he got the dirty photos, they'll only fine him for receiving stolen goods and paste the pictures on the locker room wall. And the captain will have a nice Canon outfit to take pictures at his next family shindig. So do what I tell you. Dump the pistol, then make another pass by Carver's apartment. If you find him, bring him here. If not, go home and relax. We'll regroup later. I'll call you."

After Mo departed, Brud sat by the window and started doing what he did best—working the angles. In high school in Bay Ridge, Brud had learned it was easier to crib than to study—especially when you played basketball and you had a coach who could get you off the hook. At CCNY, he had learned that the big men on campus weren't the jocks or the intellectuals. They were the guys who sold you dope—or guys like Brud who made late payers come up with the cash. In his current job, he had learned it was more profitable to take three hundred dollars under the table than five hundred over the top.

And now he was learning that if you needed a rapid infusion of cash to pay off a gambling miscalculation, you not only had to go for the big score, but you had better take care of business yourself.

Pull this off, Brud decided, and he could start coasting at the age of twenty-eight. Möet instead of Molson's. Aruba instead of Atlantic City.

First, he needed that film. Then that teenager and the photographer would have to be killed, just to keep everything tidy.

He had to get on the stick quick. He only had until Tuesday night to come up with the ten grand—it no doubt would be a couple thousand more by then with the additional interest charges. And his other partner in this scam kept bugging him—when were they going to get cracking on their latest mark? If Tracey found out they'd lost the film . . . But he wouldn't, not if Brud could help it.

Crap. Tracey's plan had sounded so easy, especially since the first few shakedowns had gone off without a hitch. And especially since this guy had sounded so perfect—real strange character, nervous just being in the West Village, skittish as a kid trying to buy his first porno magazine. It didn't require an M.B.A. to smell old money in search of new thrills. And Brud had learned enough about the guy to know he had the money to pay up—prominent Wall Street job, Tuxedo Park address, and strange notions of a good time.

The plan had come easily: Get the guy doped up, take him someplace where you had a hidden camera, put him in a compromising position, and—voilà—they'd have him exposed, framed, and nailed to the wall. What's more, with all the heavy money that Brud stood to make off the scheme, this might be Brud's ticket out of this dump, his last frame.

But they'd overlooked just how rough the West Village got after the sun went down. And there went the camera, the film, and the whole shebang.

Chapter Eight

At the station house, Will Carver bummed a panatela off a patrolman and commandeered a phone.

"Ralph? Carver. Could you send a copyboy down to the Ninth Precinct station house? Got some heavy-duty shots of a murder victim. . . . Yeah. Pawnbroker named Bingo. You heard? Well, I think I got some shots of the killer at the beginning of the roll. Could you run the film through the processor, get eight-by-tens of everything, and let me know what you got? If they're any help, we'll give 'em to the cops and give ourselves credit in print tomorrow.

"I'll leave the film with the sergeant at the front desk. I gotta file a statement and do all that bureaucratic crap, so I'll be here a while. I guess I could get out by seven to shoot Priscilla, but I don't want to put her in the middle of these gun-happy hoods. Besides, that roll you're picking up should be Page One stuff."

Ralph wanted to know what was causing the heat, but Carver changed the subject. "You find out anything on the guy in the Cherokee?"

Ralph said he'd heard that the Cherokee had been stolen from a parking garage in the Village last evening, but nothing yet on the driver.

"Too bad. Thanks. Look, sooner or later these guys are going to call back, and I want you to play along. I'm certain they're not feds at all, but I'd still like to know what their game is. . . . Maybe I'll see you later, the usual time."

After giving his statement to a pair of homicide detectives, Carver got a cup of coffee from the vending machine and told Joe

Gold what had transpired since someone had jimmied his trunk the morning before. He didn't mention the photos he had found in the stolen camera. Before he turned them over, he at least wanted to know who was in them.

He didn't have much else to do. He couldn't go to the *News*, for fear of getting shot. He couldn't go home. Somebody'd be waiting for him, no doubt. He couldn't even drive up to Riverdale and stay with an old photographer buddy. The cop who went to retrieve Carver's Rabbit said it was gone, and only masochists and pickpockets took public transit in New York.

The one thing that had gone right was that Carver's camera bag was still behind the counter in the coffee shop when a patrolman stopped by to retrieve it.

Carver left the roll of film at the front desk and retired to the narcotics room, where he'd wangled his own desk a few years back. He unlocked the top drawer and removed the pictures that seemed to be attracting half of Manhattan.

He stared at the series of eight-by-ten black-and-white photographs and tried to figure out what the fuss was about. Twelve of the twenty frames on the roll of Plus-X had been exposed, and prints of all twelve were virtually the same. Each exposure was taken from twelve feet in available light, which meant the room had been well lit for the occasion. It therefore followed that the subjects knew they were being photographed or they were too drunk or too drugged to notice.

The room looked like your basic Manhattan studio apartment—floral print chintz sofa, two ficus trees, Persian rug, and what looked to be an oak parquet tile floor. The room had two floor-to-ceiling windows with vertical blinds. A framed poster-size print of "A New Yorker's Eye View of the World" hung on the wall between the windows.

As for the subjects of the photos—a leather freak visible only from the chest down and a bimbo clad in push-up bra and lace—Carver had seen randier stuff in Times Square bookstores.

First, Carver inspected each frame for a clear view of the man, but his face always lurked just outside the frame, as if he'd looked through the lens beforehand and knew where to stand.

Carver then studied each frame for the expression on the woman's face, but it bore little information. Despite her heavy makeup, Carver could see that her eyes were glazed, a condition that applied to one-fourth of the people in Manhattan. Her lips were pursed, but Carver couldn't decide if she was smiling or wincing. From her posture—facing the camera on her hands and knees, with the man looming behind her—it was still impossible to tell if she was feeling pleasure or pain. Her hair was light colored and, judging from the blackness of her eyebrows, no doubt a dye job or a wig. That wasn't surprising for a woman in her position. Especially one who dabbled in leather, lace, and amateur photography. Probably a hooker.

Carver smelled blackmail, but one could never be certain. A cop had once offered Carver five hundred dollars to take pictures of the cop's wife fooling around with the pizza delivery boy—not to use against her in a divorce case but to blow up and hang over their king-size oval bed for inspiration. One man's fear is another man's fetish.

Carver took one more look, and got a pang of déjà vu. Maybe he'd seen her once, in a strip joint or an after-hours bar, and maybe he'd taken her picture. He wished that set of prints he was working on for the book was nearby, but they were stashed in his apartment. Maybe they could jog his memory.

At this point, he was too tired to think. He slid the photos back into the drawer, locked up, and sipped the last of the vending machine coffee. His back felt like the coffee tasted. He decided to check the books of mug shots later.

Carver reclined under the desk to get some sleep, but he was too unsettled. Maybe it was time to find a new line of employment, or at least a safer brand of photography.

He had tried studio work for a while, back when he'd first made a name for himself. He'd invested in a lot of fancy gear and set up a small studio in his kitchen, but after shooting fires and corpses, fashion layouts and food setups were too dull, too pretty, too artificial. He thrived on the fast frame—a photo shot on the fly, in the heat of battle. Not some staged shot that took hours to take, arranging the subject, shooting endless Polaroid shots to make sure the picture was composed just right before substituting an Ektachrome film magazine for the Polaroid mount and shooting the picture for keeps.

Carver had begun reading up on photography more than two decades earlier, just after he got a job as a photo lab assistant at the *News*. It was one of the few times he'd looked at a book voluntarily, and a chapter on a nineteenth-century Scottish photographer named John Thomson caught his eye.

Thomson had ventured into China to shoot a travelogue, only to discover the power of the camera along the way. When the Scotsman took photographs of villagers, they attacked him. They branded him a foreign devil—and claimed that by capturing their images on film he shortened their lives.

When Carver started to take photographs on the streets of Lower Manhattan, he discovered similar reactions. Until then, people had scarcely given him a second look. But when he aimed his camera, he might as well have wielded a gun. People froze in their tracks, hid their faces, or ducked for cover. He liked the feeling. When Carver held a camera, he was king.

For the past four years, Will Carver had spent half his nights in the station house. The Ninth was one of the hotter precincts. The crackdown around Times Square and Hell's Pantry had flushed the scum to the Lower East Side, turning the area into one of the biggest drug districts north of Little Havana.

Urbanologists called it a neighborhood in transition. Tourists called it a slum. Once a melting pot of Eastern Europeans, Turks, and immigrants from Pakistan and India, the area had slowly gone low-rent latino, with a few struggling artists for panache. In the past few years, as Manhattan real estate values soared, developers quietly poured millions into the area, figuring the gentrification to the north and west would spread.

In the meantime, abandoned tenements had become needle parlors, crack dens, and drug supermarkets, and pity the person who walked down the wrong block at night. Dealers in these parts held a grudge worse than Carver did. Horn in on their turf or double-cross them and they'd massacre your entire family, starting with the babies and working their way up to the grandmothers.

The first time Carver walked into the station house, he knew he'd found a home. The desk sergeant wore a gray bulletproof vest under her jacket, and the big room was busier than a Lotto counter on welfare check days. If a precinct house in the Bronx was called Fort Apache, this place must be the Alamo.

To Carver's left, two elderly Puerto Rican women stood before the long desk, yammering in spitfire Spanish and pointing to their open pocketbooks. A teenaged white kid, fried marbles for eyes, stood by the bank of phone directories next to the front entrance. From the snippets of conversation Carver could catch, the kid was arguing with a patrolman over whether marijuana was legal south of Fourteenth Street.

Catty-corner across the room, three clerks toiled on computers—probably inputting parking tickets. In fact, the parking ticket racket was the only task the police performed efficiently. You could find a corpse behind the wheel of a car, and the first thing a cop would do was check for money in the meter. If time had expired along with the body, he'd call for a tow truck and let someone else worry about the stiff.

Just when Carver thought the police had their act together that first night, he noticed Old Glory unfurled above the desk sergeant. Some quick arithmetic confirmed his suspicion: In the same room as the computers, they had an American flag with forty-eight stars. In the Ninth Precinct, Ike could still be president.

Carver stayed a few days, chumming around with the beat cops, walking patrol with them, and making sure they looked their best in the pictures he took of drug busts and robbery collars.

Soon after, he had a desk in the narcotics room, which sported a fifteen-foot-high ceiling and a coffee-stained floor. To the left was a holding cell the size of a zoo cage. On the far wall stood a bank of padlocked lockers. Another wall was streaked from fingerprinting-ink rollers. In the middle of the room was an island of desks, tables, and slashed vinyl chairs. Hanging from above was a light cord knotted into a noose.

Carver made himself useful, earning a few extra dollars by volunteering for police lineups uptown. The second week, he stopped—two mugging victims picked him from a lineup, and he feared he'd be arrested or asked to leave.

But the next night, two detectives were interrogating a junkie in the narcotics room at three A.M., and the guy went berserk. He flung one detective into a wall and grabbed the other's service revolver. Then he pointed it at the detective's head.

Carver, asleep under his desk as usual, was awakened by the commotion, and as he peered around the corner of the desk he managed to grasp what was going down. The guy, in jeans and bare feet, was trying to bluster his way out of the precinct house. That meant the detective who was being held prisoner was as good as embalmed. Cop law: Never let a creep walk, even if it means turning your friend's brains into a mural-size Rorschach test on the wall.

Carver scrambled to his camera bag, found his backup fifty-millimeter lens, and tried to duplicate his Philly schoolyard form. He reared back, took aim, and let fly a rocket.

It caught the junkie on the base of the skull. As he staggered, the gun discharged and blood splattered. In the ensuing chaos, the cops jumped the addict and pummeled his face until you couldn't tell which bloodstains on the floor belonged to him and which belonged to the fallen cop.

As far as the officers of the Ninth Precinct were concerned, the night had a happy ending. The addict was found hanging from the bars of the holding cell the next morning.

The detective survived and got reassigned to the bomb squad, on the assumption it was easier to handle hair-trigger explosives than hair-trigger junkies.

As for Carver, he had himself a front-page photo in the *Daily News*—and a home for himself in the station house for as long as he wanted to sleep on the floor.

The way things were shaping up, Carver would be spending another night on the linoleum mattress. A messenger from the *News* dropped off the prints of the roll that Carver had shot that morning, and Carver had come up empty. The photos of Bingo were on the money, but a ten-year-old could have taken those. The pictures Carver wanted were ones of the fleeing killer, and they didn't offer much more than the cops already knew. Suspect was a male Caucasian, thirty to forty years old, between five-foot-eight and five-foot-ten. Dark red hair, stocky build, cowboy jacket, polyester pants.

At Joe Gold's request, Carver went through several books of mug shots. By the time he finished and headed for some shut-eye in the narcotics room, he figured he'd looked at a thousand photos. He recognized ten men in the photos. Each of them was one of Carver's acquaintances.

Chapter Nine

"Will, wake up. Time to go home."

Carver rolled over and squinted, but the top of the desk blocked his view. It had to be Gina. Nobody else called him anything but "Hey, you" or Carver.

"Gimme a few minutes more."

"Let's go, Will. It's late, I'm off duty, and I'm more tired than you are."

Carver climbed out from under the desk and tried to stand. His back ached. Again.

"Even if I wanted to leave here, I can't," he said, pulling himself to his feet. "I've managed to get myself in the middle of a mess, and I figure that long about now my place is a convention center for thugs."

"I heard you were in a jam," Gina replied. "I meant my place."

"Hadn't thought of that." Carver paused a moment to shake off his drowsiness. "But I couldn't, even if I wanted to. I'm sure somebody's waiting for me outside."

"Your decision, Will. If you want to make yourself a prisoner here, that's your business. You seem to like it. But if you'd rather go to my place, I suggest you get moving."

"And how am I going to do that without getting my head shot off?"

"You got a peacoat, right? So get cleaned up, borrow some blue slacks and a patrolman's hat. Nobody will look at you twice. Besides, it's eleven P.M. Even hoodlums take Friday nights off."

Carver nodded yes and removed a Bic razor from the desk. As

he headed toward the men's room, he couldn't help but think that things were looking up for the first time in ages. For the past four years, Gina had been a voice on the phone, one of the many police dispatchers Carver relied on for news tips—at twenty dollars a pop. Until now, he hadn't thought of her as a member of the opposite sex, just an inside line to the Ninth Precinct.

He remembered that she was single, a widow or something, but he'd been too busy to think of her beyond work. His mistake: He now tried to picture her out of uniform, and liked what he saw. Five-foot-seven, high cheekbones, nice figure, flowing black hair—the kind that takes a half-hour to brush. From the crow's feet around her eyes and the creases on her neck, no spring chicken. But then he was no cock of the walk.

Carver recalled how pleasant she'd always been, and now it was all adding up. Although most women thought him strange, he would occasionally get lucky. Some women actually found his job glamorous. Some women just weren't too choosy.

Gina fell somewhere in between. Definitely available. Maybe a bit lonesome, although he'd never get her to admit it. Probably didn't want to fool around with cops but didn't get much chance to meet men outside the station house. And there arrived Carver . . . available, willing, and, as one girlfriend had described him, "educable."

A cold and steady rain fell as Gina Constantine and Carver left the station house, and an umbrella provided as good a cover as the improvised uniform as they headed north on Second Avenue. Five minutes later, they reached Gina's apartment above a bookstore on St. Marks Place. Carver's right knee clicked on the stairs. He shrugged when Gina asked about it. Truth was, Carver was getting older and he didn't want to admit it to a woman he planned on bedding.

Gina's place was cold and damp. She adjusted the thermostat as they entered, and she offered to go for take-out Chinese food while the place warmed up. After she left, Carver removed his wet shoes, slid them under the living room radiator, and gave Gina's place a quick inspection. Not bad on police pay. Wall-to-wall carpeting, white Indian cotton sofa, hanging plants, fresh flowers on the glass coffee table. Beside the vase sat an issue of

Redbook. Not a good sign: Carver wished it were a *Cosmopolitan.* Underneath was Gina's latest New York Telephone bill. Since the envelope already had been opened, Carver removed the contents and inspected the long-distance calls. Three calls to Long Island, two to a number in Maryland. If Gina had a serious boyfriend, Carver concluded, the guy must live in Manhattan.

The kitchen, with a yellow formica dinette set, occupied a corner of the room. The table and chairs looked secondhand, but this sort of junk was fashionable these days and Gina probably'd paid good money for it. Two years before, he'd seen a similar set left for trash on a Chelsea side street.

He opened the door to the bedroom. Antique brass-and-iron bed with a beige goose-down comforter. An old cedar chest for a nightstand. Atop it sat a nine-inch TV and a gold-framed photo of a laughing young policeman. Carver decided to think positive. Maybe the cop was her brother.

Carver opened the closet. Eighteen pairs of shoes sat neatly in a vinyl contraption that hung inside the door. The closet itself was crammed with dresses and blouses. He flipped through them, trying to get a sense of Gina's taste in clothing, when he came across the patrolman's uniform: Gina definitely had a boyfriend in New York after all.

Carver felt a pang in his chest and closed the door in a hurry. The last thing he wanted was to get mixed up with a woman who was mixed up with someone else. "Mixed up" was the perfect term for it. He'd been on the wrong end of that game once before. . . . He tried to think of something else before he started to dwell on it the way he used to. The memories still cut deep.

More to the point, all he needed now was for the cop boyfriend to arrive. Upon brief reflection, he decided that it was unlikely—Gina wouldn't be inviting Carver over if her boyfriend were going to show up at any moment. Carver walked to the bed, gave it a solid thump with the palm of his right hand to check the firmness of the mattress, and thought about what might lie in store. He inhaled deeply and noticed a trace of lavender in the air.

That was the major difference between men and women, Carver decided. Men's bedrooms, or at least his bedroom, stank of day-old cigar butts. Women's smelled like an Avon lady's sample case.

Alas, the last time he'd been in a woman's bedroom for any length of time was when he'd begun dating his ex-wife, and the memories came creeping back. It was the summer of 'seventy-four, the middle of a heat wave, and she had a walk-up on East Eighteenth Street. They'd been to a rock concert at the Wollman Rink in Central Park, and it was still eighty degrees when they arrived at her brownstone at eleven P.M. Inside wasn't much cooler. The air conditioner was in her bedroom.

She smiled and said, "Don't get any ideas," then led him inside. She switched on the air conditioner. As she reached for the light, Carver embraced her and they fell under some strange physical spell that seemed murky, unwholesome, inevitable. Hands slipped down collars and between buttons, cat burglars tiptoeing through half-open doors.

Elastic stretched, clasps unclinched, and Carver felt the cool breeze of the softly descending cotton bedsheet. Love at first sex.

A week later, they took a long lunch hour and wed downtown in a civil ceremony. Carver later joked it was the only civil thing about the marriage.

The door clicked open. "See anything you like?"

Carver turned with a start. "Sorry, Gina. Just wanted to make sure we didn't have company. Maybe you ought to know right off the bat that I'm a classic neurotic. But as the saying goes, just because I'm paranoid doesn't mean I'm not being followed."

"You're right, Will. Only neurotics talk in double negatives. Why don't you cool it? Nobody followed us. I would have noticed when I went out for our dinner. So relax."

The two arranged the white containers of Chinese food on the dinette and ate in silence, as though they were a long-married couple. Carver could taste the salty traces of chemicals in the beef with snow peas, but he was too hungry to complain. Besides, the beef would have been as tough as horsehide without the monosodium glutamate. The latest in life's long line of trade-offs.

After finishing a second helping, Carver put his plate in the sink.

"My back is killing me," Carver said. "Mind if I lie down for a few minutes, or is that being forward?"

"Not at all. In fact, take a shower while I change my clothes, then I'll give you a rubdown if you like. I have witch hazel in the medicine cabinet."

"Sounds good. I'll take off my clothes if you take off yours."

"Whoa, buddy," Gina said. "Don't go making assumptions. I'm offering a massage. Period."

Carver walked into the bedroom, took off his shirt, and lay facedown on the mattress. His body sank three inches. "You know, Gina, you really oughtta get a board for this."

"Why? I hope you're not planning on coming back."

He cricked his head around just in time to see Gina unclasp her bra.

Gina covered up, but not before he got a look. As she hastily donned a robe, he called after her: "No need to get modest on my account."

"Stow it," she said. "I thought you'd have the decency not to turn around."

"Me and decency mentioned in the same breath? Stop the presses. We got a first here."

"And no doubt a last." Gina scowled. "You think all single women want to hop in the sack at the drop of an insult? I'm not that desperate."

"Guess I had you pegged wrong. I mean, you are a single woman. You did invite me over at eleven P.M., and it's a little late for a game of cards. I thought maybe after hanging around with cops all these years, you'd see me as a breath of fresh air."

"Stop right there. Let's get something straight. Don't go knocking policemen around me. I like cops. Got that?"

"Is that why you've got a cop's uniform hanging in your closet—in case your patrolman pal sleeps over?"

Gina folded her arms across her chest and glowered. "That was my husband's uniform. He was a cop, and he got killed because of it."

Carver tried to muster a reply, but Gina kept talking over him. "And after he died, I stayed on at the station house because his friends were good to me. But I don't have to explain anything to you. Besides, you had no business snooping in my closet. What the hell do you think you're doing?"

"Looking for prowlers," Carver said, then stood and walked to the bureau. Gina thought he was going to look at her husband's picture. He flicked on the TV set instead.

"Now what are you doing?"

"Thought there might be an old 'Kojak' episode on, seeing as how you like cops so much."

Gina extended her middle finger, wheeled, and left the room.

When the TV warmed up, a talk show came on. The host and a woman guest were discussing extramarital sex. Carver rolled over and went to sleep.

Chapter Ten

SATURDAY MORNING

Will Carver awoke to the sound of a bureau drawer sliding shut. After he got his bearings, he raised his head in time to see Gina buttoning her blouse.

He remembered the unfinished business of the night before. "I got it, Gina. I'll give you the backrub."

Gina ignored the comment. "It's ten A.M. You had your safe place to sleep. So why don't you just get up and get out? You don't interest me."

"Then why keep undressing while I'm in the room? Give me a tumble. You didn't ask me over for chitchat."

"Give me a break. You were in a jam and needed a place to crash. What makes you think I want your body? Maybe I'm just a soft touch for homeless mutts, Will. You've known me for how long? Four years? And you've never said more than 'Hi, where's the murder?' "

"I didn't want to ruin a fine professional relationship," Carver countered, and sat up on the bed. "And it never occurred to me you'd fall for a slob."

"I haven't, believe me. Besides, your unkempt appearance is a big act. But you know that better than I do. You don't have to dress like an overturned dumpster in order to do your job."

"That's what you think," he said, sneaking a quick look at his fingernails to see if they were clean. "Nobody looks twice at an overturned dumpster in New York City, and that's what I want. It's tough enough shooting psychopaths and derelicts. If I dress like the Brooks Brothers or L. L. Bean or Calvin Klein on safari, wackos would go for my lens—or my neck."

When he looked up, Gina had turned away to tuck her pale blue oxford cloth blouse into her jeans. She appeared distracted as she looked in the dresser mirror, and Carver wasn't sure if she was paying attention.

Gina applied some lipstick before replying. "So what's your point? Why worry about wackos? Look at what you have now. Thugs shooting your best friend and ransacking your apartment. No offense, but isn't it time you ended the longest running show on the Bowery? Will Carver, low-rent photographer. I mean, you look like a poster boy for Goodwill Industries. Why dress like that?"

Carver rubbed his chin and felt a few whiskers he'd missed when he'd shaved at the station house. He kept his hand on his chin to hide them. "I guess there are three reasons why I dress the way I do. The first is I'm Scottish, and the stereotype is true—I'm cheap. Second, nice clothes embarrass me. I look at guys in fancy tailored suits and I think, How can they squander money on such superficial crap? I see a big shot lawyer with a thousand-dollar Rolex, and I know what time it is. It's time for the rich bastard to examine his values in life. The richer you are, the more bankrupt you get.

"Finally, if you'll pardon the sermonette, I want people to judge me for what I am, not for what I wear. People who don't like me because of the way I dress aren't worth knowing."

"Maybe they're just afraid of fleas," Gina said. "Sorry. Cheap shot. Let's drop it. But meanwhile, you still haven't told me what really happened yesterday, or was it the day before?"

That got Carver stirring. "You buy today's *Daily News*?"

"Yes, and a couple containers of coffee. I hope you take it black. If not, I think I have some milk. . . ."

Carver wasn't paying attention. He bolted from the bed, wrapped a sheet around his waist, and reached for the newspaper sitting on the dresser.

He'd made the front page:

BOWERY BLOODBATH

Typical *Daily News* hype. But he had to hand it to them—they still knew how to sell newspapers. And they'd used the shot of Bingo on Page One. Carver flipped to Page Three and saw an old mug shot of himself, plus a story with his byline. No mention of dirty photographs, his ransacked apartment, his missing car. If you believed the *News*, he'd simply wandered into Bingo's in the midst of World War III.

Carver flipped the paper onto the coffee table and complained: "Did you read this? One half-truth after another. The only accurate thing in the whole piece is that I'm under protective custody."

Gina walked to the window and looked out onto St. Marks Place, which was beginning to fill with the usual Saturday tourists looking for cheap jewelry and other assorted junk.

Finally, she turned back toward Carver and broke her silence. "Will, far be it from me to defend the *Daily News*, but they only embellished the statement you gave Joe Gold. I saw the copyboy slip Joe a twenty-dollar bill, and I assume it was for a copy of whatever you told him."

"Great," Carver countered. "I get a byline, he gets a twenty. And Joe's supposed to be a friend. No telling what he'd do for a grand."

"Come on," Gina said, and walked to the sofa. "That's not what's bothering you. Fess up."

"Okay, dammit. I'm mad because they ran my picture."

"So?"

"So I like to maintain a low profile."

Gina pressed him: "Come on, there has to be more to it than that."

"If you must know, I hate having my picture in the paper because the only people who get their photos published are jocks, crooks, politicians, and slain coeds, and they're not the company I want to keep."

"Go on."

"And some twit poodle is probably squatting on my photograph now," he said. "Don't you see? Newspapers are dirty if you're on the wrong end of them. Hell, Bloomingdale's sells little white gloves to people who want to read the *Times* without soiling their hands. And that's for the *Times*. Can you imagine what they'd sell for the *Post*?"

"Sure, Will. Oven mitts. You've made your point, I guess, but there's more to your irritation over the photo than you're letting on."

Carver tapped his fingers on the newspaper for effect. "Newspapers make their money by airing other people's underwear. If you're in the paper, you're in the public domain. Open season. Some Middle Eastern religions believe it's a sin to have your picture taken. They believe that when somebody takes your picture, he takes part of your soul. Get down to it, they're right."

Gina had heard enough. "Yeah, and you're the one who's taking the pictures. How do you justify that? But enough of your bizarre theories, Will. What do you do now?"

"Does it matter?" He didn't know where to begin. Finally, he told Gina the whole story, from the dying words of the guy in the Jeep Cherokee to the gunfight at Bingo's.

"What can I do?" he said. "I show my face on the street, I'll probably catch a bullet from a passing car. And I won't even know who's shooting at me. I've got an assortment of dirty photos, but I don't know who's in them, where they were taken, when, or by whom. I don't even know who to return them to. I guess I have to find the kid. Bingo said the name of the kid who stole the camera was the Puma. Bingo even gave me an address."

"You'd be better off going to the police."

"I don't have anything for them to go on yet."

"Then how can I help?"

"Have any picture-hanging wire?"

"Let me check. I think I have some in the kitchen drawer. Anything else?"

"Go back to the station house, return the slacks and hat, and borrow a flak jacket for me. Please."

When Gina heard that, she returned to the window and tried to hide her agitation. To keep her hands busy, she pinched back a Swedish Ivy, the one houseplant that required more maintenance than the Studebaker Lark that Carver once owned. He recognized the plant instantly—he used to give them as presents to people he wanted to irritate.

When Gina spoke again, she talked into the plant rather than look at him. "I'd be happy to go to the station house for you, but you still ought to stay out of the line of fire. While you're at it, you should think this whole thing through. If you can't sell the pictures, why are you a threat to anyone?"

He didn't reply. Gina finally turned to face him. "Tell you what. Think it over, and I'll run that errand after my exercise class. You might as well stay till nightfall. You won't find the kid till then anyway. If it's open season on anyone connected with that roll of film, the kid's gone to ground."

"Okay, I'll stay," he said. "But only if you let me watch you button your blouse again."

"I doubt you'd find that the least bit erotic unless you were watching from the fire escape, secretly taking pictures for your private portfolio. Why must you filter your experiences through a thirty-five-millimeter camera?"

"Because the Speed Graphic got too heavy."

Carver felt Round Two coming on, and Gina delivered. "Knock it off. I've seen your photographs in the papers often enough. You're drawn to disaster, but instead of helping save people, you take their picture."

"You got me all wrong."

Gina interrupted. "Fat chance. Take the shot of the murdered pawnbroker in today's paper. He was your friend, and you got there moments after he'd been shot, right? And did you stop taking pictures long enough to call an ambulance?"

Before he replied, Carver paused a moment to find his Phillies cap in his jacket pocket. The cap was the closest thing to a security blanket he had this side of a cigar, and he felt more at ease the moment he put it on. "I'm sorry, Gina, but photographers get paid to take pictures. Period. If you're in a combat zone, you take your pictures, then worry about the wounded. Otherwise newspapers would hire medics instead of photographers, stories would run without pictures, and nobody would read them."

"You don't really believe that."

Carver tugged at the brim of his cap, locked eyes with Gina, and continued. "I don't see CARE's name on my paycheck, do I? What did Shakespeare say? You gotta be cruel to be kind.

Look, when I started out, I did all the rinkydink jobs—ribbon cuttings, press conferences. One time an editor at the *Post* asks me to go over to Bellevue and shoot a picture of an abandoned baby. When I get there, a nurse brings out the cutest little foundling. I'm about to take the picture, but the nurse says wait. She takes out a pin and jabs the baby's foot, and the kid screams to high heaven.

"Now take the picture, she says. When I'm done, I ask why she pricked the baby with that pin. Know what she said? That the reason I'm there is to take a picture for this baby's mother to see in the paper. If the baby looks too contented, the mother'll feel she's done the right thing. But when she sees her baby screaming, she'll feel terrible. And then she'll come get her baby."

Gina shook her head from side to side: "Nice try, but you don't photograph abandoned babies anymore. . . . Never mind. We're getting nowhere. I'm going. See you in an hour or two."

After Gina left, Carver brooded. He felt out of place, as though he were in a doctor's waiting room without an appointment. So he sat there, trying to figure how to get Gina to hop into the sack. Maybe now that they'd gotten to know each other, talked like real grown-ups. . . . In a few minutes, he gave up; he decided he'd find warmer women in the morgue.

He picked up the *Daily News* again and opened to the obituary page. It was a tough place to keep track of your friends.

Chapter Eleven

Brud Siracusa had awakened at seven-thirty and braced himself for the long Saturday ahead by going through his usual morning routine. Wheat germ and vitamins for breakfast, washed down with orange juice, then a solid twenty-minute workout on the rowing machine. After showering, he went out for his daily papers. He wasn't big on current events, but hope sprang eternal every weekend on the sports pages, where the morning line on the college and pro football games was printed as religiously as the horoscope. In truth, Brud believed they often went hand in hand, save for the fact that whereas no one could throw a horoscope, one could certainly throw a football game.

His mood was so upbeat that a look at the pawnbroker's picture on the front page of the *Daily News* provided only fleeting concern. After all, the pawnbroker was dead, and there was nothing Brud could do to change it. And if there was nothing he could do to change it, then it wasn't a problem. That was the only wisdom he had gleaned from years of therapy, but it was good advice at any price.

More important were today's big college games, which held the promise of helping him extricate himself from his current jam. If he could pick a winner and come up with a few grand, he'd be able to buy himself more time. Sitting at the breakfast table in his Village high rise, he spread out the sports sections from the *Post*, the *News*, and *Newsday*. He scanned all the hype stories on the various games—USC–Notre Dame, West Virginia–Syracuse, Michigan–Ohio State—and looked for some magic information on which to make his wager.

He jotted down the point spreads on a yellow legal pad that he had swiped from the office, then turned to the weather page to see what game conditions were likely to be. He kept going back to one game, West Virginia at Syracuse, and saw an upset in the making. West Virginia had been on a roll, but Syracuse was tough in the Carrier Dome. Plus there was the slight bias he had for a team with the same last name as his. West Virginia was favored by a point. Easy money.

To get a second opinion, he read all the horoscope columns. One of the astrological forecasts for Aries cinched the bet: "You'll take greater charge of your own destiny. Financial picture will clear up if you stay close to home. Added responsibility may create the feeling of being trapped. Benefits outweigh temporary disadvantage."

Now all he had to do was find a bookie willing to give him a line of credit and take his bet. Billy Bones, his regular bookie, was out of the question. Brud's bad bets with Billy had put him in his current mess in the first place. He leafed through his address book, then dialed his cordless phone.

"Hello, John. Brud Siracusa here. I want to place a couple grand on the Syracuse–West Virginia game. Is the spread still West Virginia by a point? Fine. I'd like to put two thou on Syracuse. My credit's good, right?"

Click.

Brud dialed two other numbers, with the same results. The fourth bookmaker stayed on the phone long enough to confirm Brud's suspicions. "The word's out, Brud. You're a bad credit risk. Billy Bones says you were into him for ten grand, and your loan shark says you can't pay up. I don't need the aggravation. So unless you want to go cash-and-carry on this one, you're out of luck."

Brud hung up the phone and rubbed the cut on his cheek. The horoscope was right. The time had come to take greater charge of his destiny.

Chapter Twelve

Will Carver left Gina's apartment at noon and walked the ten blocks north to Stuyvesant Town, a phalanx of red-brick apartment buildings to the north of Alphabet City. The slow, cold rain had settled in for the weekend, and Carver's Phillies cap soon soaked through.

At the corner of Fourteenth Street and Avenue A, he stopped at the window of a candy store, wiped the rain from his forehead, and checked his appearance in the glass's reflection. He knew before he looked that he looked like hell. He had never sat shiva before, but he knew that a two-day-old white shirt and faded jeans would be inappropriate under any circumstance. In this situation, it only made bad matters worse. Still, all he could do was hope that Bingo's sister would understand that Carver couldn't let friendships come before duty.

He cringed at the lameness of his logic: Not only had he taken pictures of Bingo moments after he died, but Carver had had the gall to peddle them to a tabloid.

Carver entered the sprawling apartment complex, taking the curved macadam path past the barren pin oak trees and dogwoods, where pigeons roosted motionless on branches under the steady rain. In the suburbs, this would be another drab set of medium-rise apartment buildings. In New York City, it was an oasis.

Carver walked up the four slate steps to Seven Stuyvesant Oval and pushed open the glass door. In the tiny entrance, he went to the mailboxes to check Pearl's intercom number, then dialed.

"Who is it?" Carver barely recognized Pearl's voice on the house phone.

"It's Will Carver."

"Will Carver? Will Carver?" She was shouting now. "How dare you? Go away."

"I want to explain...."

"I don't have time for your explanations. Now go away before I call the police."

Carver turned to leave, but couldn't. He thought about the other times he had come to call here, when Bingo and his sister had given him his first home-cooked meal in months and made him stay to watch television with them.

Carver felt more at home there than he did at his apartment, except for when Pearl would take a sip of her after-dinner sherry and announce, "What you need, WillCarver"—she pronounced his name as one three-syllable word, WillCarver—"what you need is a good woman."

And Carver would sigh and reply, "Pearl, we've been through this a hundred times. I was married once, and I don't want to go through that nightmare ever again."

Pearl would ask Bingo to turn down the TV, then she'd go through her usual sales pitch: "You eat one burnt potato chip and you throw out the entire bag? There's plenty of nice young women out there that would love to have a catch like you."

And Carver would tell Bingo to turn the volume on the TV up again, Pearl would roll her eyes, and they'd all have a good laugh over it.

Carver trembled at the memory. Pearl and Bingo were as close to family as Carver had ever had, and he had betrayed them. He had been an idiot to come here, but now he found himself unable to walk away.

He stared out into the rain until he lost track of time. Why did he have to take Bingo's picture? Why did he have to sell it? He used to be able to answer questions like that off the top of his head, but the answers sounded so hollow now. Why did he have to become a newspaper photographer?

His mind raced with questions, but he could come up with no answers. Finally, he pressed his forehead against the cold windowpane, in hopes it would numb his brain.

A voice behind him shook him from his trance. "Sir, can I help you?"

Carver turned around. It was a janitor. Carver decided he had nothing to lose. "I'm here to pay my last respects to a friend, Pearl Barolsky up on the fourth floor, but her intercom doesn't seem to work. Can you let me in?"

The janitor shrugged and unlocked the door that led to the elevators.

Outside Pearl's apartment, Carver put his Phillies cap in his peacoat pocket and tapped on the door. His hand was shaking.

An old man in a dark suit answered the door. "Come in. Who shall I say is calling?"

Carver's throat was dry, and the words came hard. "I can't come in. But could you please tell Pearl that Will Carver came to pay his last respects? Tell her I'm sorry, and I hope one day she'll find it in her heart to forgive me."

Then he turned away and headed to the elevator. When he reached the front door, he wiped his eyes, looked up toward the sky, and saw that the rain was still falling outside, too.

Chapter Thirteen

As Brud Siracusa hung up the phone in his West Fourth Street office, he felt like the PR man at Three Mile Island. Yes, there's been a spill. We have it contained. No problem. No danger. No sweat.

Still, Brud began to wonder.

He clicked open the gold cigarette case, a present from his uncle, and extracted a French cigarette with a name he couldn't quite pronounce. It had a dark brown wrapper and smelled like burning rubber, but it was part of the continental image Brud liked to project, so he put up with the aroma. Brud sat at his desk and collected his thoughts until the cigarette burned down to the filter, then he walked over to the window.

It was two P.M., but with the rain it might as well have been dusk. With the heel of his palm, Brud wiped the condensation from the window before him. On the street below, taxis whizzed past with their headlights on, and umbrellas bobbed on the sidewalk. Sloppy day, sloppy business.

Brud drew the blinds and started to pace. He was running out of money and running out of time—and growing tired of the waiting game with the damned photographer. Mo had checked out Carver's apartment last night and this morning and once more had come up empty. And Brud himself had wasted an hour waiting for Carver at the News Building last night—even paid a copyboy twenty bucks to call if Carver showed up.

When Brud had answered the phone a few minutes earlier, he had hoped the caller would be that copyboy. Instead, it was Tracey, pissed as hell. Actually, the conversation had gone well,

Brud decided, in light of how bitchy his partner could get when things fell short of perfect. Brud had figured that Mo must have said something to tip Tracey off, and that he might as well just tell the truth, then stonewall like crazy: We lost the film. We know who's got it. We're in the process of getting it back. Give us one more day, then we'll put the screws to our patsy. That's a promise.

Tracey had no choice but to go along.

At two-thirty, Brud Siracusa convened the pep talk for Mo. Big money was at stake, and Mo had better get on the stick or they might as well forget the whole damned scheme.

Staring across the desk at Mo, Brud realized he had better keep this chat brief and hard-assed. Mo had only three things going for him: He was loyal, he worked cheap, and he enjoyed hitting people.

Brud had learned that ten years earlier, when he and Mo used the same boxing gym on Fourteenth Street. Brud had gone there because a basketball coach had said that learning to box would help his coordination, foot speed, and endurance. At the gym, located above a pool hall off Union Square, Brud had learned much more—like how to use a shiv, how to hotwire a car, how to throw a sucker punch when somebody called him a pretty boy.

The day Brud met Mo, Brud had gotten into an argument with a hotheaded Hispanic kid over who would use the light bag. Brud thought he'd won the discussion, only to get decked from behind. Next thing Brud knew, the kid was on top of him, pummeling his face. Brud couldn't remember which punch had broken his nose, but he was semiconscious when Mo arrived out of nowhere and hammered the kid so hard on the side of the head that he knocked the kid out cold.

After a trainer inspected Brud's nose and told him he might as well get used to it, Brud introduced himself to Mo and bought him a beer at a dive down the block. They'd been buddies and sometime business associates ever since.

Mo used to work as a sparring partner for a few light heavyweights, until he'd taken so many shots to the head that his opponents were afraid they'd throw the punch that would kill him.

Since then, Mo had gotten by working as a bouncer and doing bill-collection work for Brud.

Over the years, Brud learned that you never let Mo make decisions, you never double-crossed him, and you never let him stray too far. At this point, Brud had to ask Mo to work on his own again, and that was dangerous—especially with the state that Mo was in. Brud figured the cause must be that picture in today's *Daily News*. Brud had convinced Mo that the cops weren't after him, but even a punch-drunk guy like Mo had enough sense to know that the photo was bad publicity for the cops and they'd be working overtime on the case.

Brud decided to press forward, keep Mo's mind off yesterday. "I know we've had a run of bad luck, Mo, but we're going to change that tonight.

"Here's the game plan, nice and simple. I'm going to pay our friendly photographer a visit at the *Daily News*. I checked again with his contact there, and he's supposed to stop by at six to pick up some negatives and a paycheck. I think the guy bought my story that I needed to talk to Carver about the circumstances surrounding Tony's death Thursday night, so there shouldn't be a problem."

Mo nodded halfheartedly. He was still thinking about the front page of the *Daily News*.

Brud snapped his fingers to get Mo's attention. "Meanwhile, pal, I need you to go over to the East Village and find the kid who stole our camera. Check with the street people, see where the kid hangs out. A young mugger with a name like Puma Jefferson shouldn't be hard to track down. When you find him, kill him. I don't care how, just keep it neat."

Mo asked if there'd be a bonus involved, and Brud slammed his fist on the desk. "No, Mo, let's make this job on the house. You need him dead as much as I do. If the cops ever get hold of him, the kid might make the connection between us and Bingo's Pawnshop. The kid can read the papers as well as you can."

Mo scratched his beer gut. "I'm confused, Brud. How could the kid connect us with the pawnshop?"

"The camera bag had my name tag on it, remember? I know, it was stupid on my part, but I didn't plan on it getting stolen—

let alone with the damned film inside. If the kid made a mental note of my name and address before he chucked the bag, we're screwed."

"How do you know he chucked the bag?"

"I'm guessing that he's not going to keep anything that can tie him to a mugging. And one more thing. Keep an eye out for Carver. If the pawnbroker gave us the kid's name, he probably told Carver, too. Carver may be looking for the kid to see what he knows about the camera. So be ready."

Mo scrunched his face. "And what do I do if I see Carver?"

"Bring him here."

"What if he don't wanna come?"

"That's why I pay you the big bucks," Brud snapped. "Just don't kill him until we get our hands on the film."

Time to stay cool, Brud reminded himself. Talk positive, and positive things happen. He took a cigarette from the case, lit it, and inhaled deeply. He held the smoke in his lungs for a few seconds, then exhaled through his nose the way he'd seen in old gangster flicks.

"This guy Carver won't be a problem," Brud said. "I guarantee it. He got lucky once or twice, but he's scared stiff. We have all the advantages. He doesn't know who we are, what the pictures are all about, or when we're gonna strike. So let's just get out there and get the job done."

After Mo had trudged out, Brud sat back and took a swig of take-out coffee that was two hours cold. It tasted awful, but he needed the caffeine to keep him wired.

Brud sensed the scam slipping out of reach. Mo was the weak link. He'd follow orders only so long as everything went according to plan. Otherwise he was worse than worthless. What was the expression? Loose cannon? Yeah, Mo, was a loose cannon on the deck of the good ship Blackmail, and the ship was springing leaks.

Nothing fatal, at least not yet. Puma was obviously some street punk—Mo could handle him no sweat. It was the photographer who had Brud worried. As long as Carver had the film, he had them by the balls.

Chapter Fourteen

There's an old fortune cookie proverb that goes: "Even dirt glitters when the sun is shining." In Manhattan, it works a little differently.

At night, after a rain, the city gleams. Neon signs and street lamps and headlights shine on the wet pavement, to the point where you don't notice the garbage cans chained to lampposts and the litter in the gutters. The derelicts disappear in search of a dry place to sit with their rotgut, and the city seems brand-new.

The fresh air lifted Will Carver's spirits as he set out for Alphabet City. He was armed with a name and an address, a bulletproof vest, and a loop of picture-hanging wire wrapped inside the brim of his Phillies cap. Although East Fifth Street off Avenue B was a short walk from Gina's flat, his trip took on the air of an expedition. If Bingo had told the thugs where to reach the kid, chances were that somebody was waiting.

Carver wasn't going in totally cold. He'd phoned Allie, a young artist buddy who ran a gallery on East Fourth, and asked him to check the area, put some feelers out for the Puma, and look for any cars circling the block or hanging around the Puma's apartment building.

The reply hadn't been encouraging. According to Allie, some kids who knew the Puma said he'd be home around six, and a 'sixty-eight Nova had been spotted several times—parked across the street from the Puma's place, and a few more times driving past the gallery. Allie said the driver was no tourist. He was circling like a vulture.

Carver was three buildings from the Puma's place when he saw the Nova approach. He bent to tie a shoelace, but the driver had spotted him. The car hesitated twenty feet away. He wondered if it could be the same guy who ran out of Bingo's the day before.

Carver's mind raced. Why didn't anything come easy? If he tried to beat a fast retreat, he could expect a bullet in the back. If he stayed put much longer, the guy'd come after him on foot. The street was empty, save for an old lady walking her dog halfway down the block.

He who hesitates is dead, he decided, and made his move. He rolled behind a parked van and came up running. He heard a car door behind him, a voice yelling "Stop," then a metal apartment house door clicking open ahead of him on the left. As he lunged for it, he felt a slug hit him in the shoulder, propelling him through the half-open doorway and into a young Puerto Rican woman.

Showing no etiquette, Carver pushed her against a row of mail slots and tried the inside door. Locked. He grabbed the woman's keys from her hand. Her mouth was open but no words sprang forth.

A key fit on first try, and Carver left the woman frozen in the doorway. By the time he'd reached the first landing, she had overcome her shock and was screaming bloody mayhem. At the second landing, her cries hit a shriller pitch. Somebody was chasing him.

He lit out for the top floor and prayed that the door to the roof was unlocked. It was. He was home free—compared to a minute ago, at least.

Fighting the darkness, he ran as best he could across the flat tar-paper-and-gravel roof and jumped across a small alley to the next roof, then repeated the maneuver. When he felt he was out of harm's path, he took shelter behind a stairwell. His knee was swollen. His back throbbed.

But he decided that things could be worse. First, he had a secure hiding place. Second, the thug must be figuring him for dying or dead. The slug he took in the back would have killed any normal man, or any normal man not wearing a flak jacket.

If he had to take up with a woman again, Carver concluded, one who worked for the police had the edge.

For five minutes, Carver listened for footsteps on the rooftops.

But it wasn't until another five minutes elapsed, and he heard the sirens, that he realized he was safe. Figuring it would take another ten minutes for the police to talk the story out of the woman and look for his body, Carver started to look for an escape route.

A police escort to the station house had a comforting ring, but getting them involved was like asking an in-law for advice. What you wanted and what you ended up with were two different matters.

Besides, he could accomplish more on the street, especially if he'd been left for dead.

Carver looked for a way to reach his friend's art gallery, but the buildings across the courtyard were twenty yards away, and no phone wire or clothesline would hold his weight. Circumnavigating the rooftops was out of the question, too. At both ends of the block stood ten-story buildings, bookends propping up a shelf of tired row homes.

Finally, he realized that the Puma's apartment house couldn't be but a few rooftops away. He counted from Avenue B, multiplied by two, and concluded the next roof was the one.

There was a drop of about ten feet, so he bent over, grabbed the roof's edge, and landed unceremoniously in a puddle about six inches deep. The door on the roof pried open without trouble. Moments later he parked himself outside the door to apartment G-4.

Nobody answered his knock, so he sat halfway up the next flight of stairs and waited. His teeth chattered. After fifteen minutes, Carver removed his work shoes, wrung out his socks, and hung them on the banister to dry.

They were still soaked when he heard footsteps approach the apartment below.

He stood and softly descended the stairs in time to see a three-hundred-pound black teenager put a key in the door.

"Know where I might find the Puma?" Carver asked.

"Don't know who you're talkin' 'bout, man."

As the kid walked into his apartment, Carver saw the untied high-topped black sneakers and followed them through the door.

"Relax, Puma," Carver said. "I'm a friend of Bingo's, and I'm here to save both our butts."

Chapter Fifteen

"What you want with me, man? I'm busy."

"It's like this," Will Carver said. "You may not realize it, but you and me are up crap's creek in the same canoe."

"You lost me, man. I think it's time you leave."

Puma was sitting on the sofa, or most of it. He wore a Run DMC T-shirt and expensive jeans. From where Carver stood, a few feet away, Puma's girth seemed so enormous that Carver couldn't tell if the kid was about to get up or settled in for the night.

Before he could decide, Carver heard a noise outside the door. In an instant, he reached into his cap brim for the wire noose. In the next instant, he went flying butt-over-belly across the carpet. He rose to see a woman in the doorway, pointing a gun at his head.

"Joey said you had company, Oradell."

"It's okay, Mom. I think he's friendly. And if he's not, I'll deck him again."

"Sorry if I gave you a scare, ma'am," Carver said as he tried to stand. "I was about to talk to Oradell here about our mutual interest in photography. There's no problem. No problem whatsoever."

"Oradell?" The woman turned to Puma for reassurance.

"It's cool, Mom," he said. "Put that piece away. Besides, what you doin' with my gun? You been cleanin' my room or what?"

"Oradell, I told you I don't like you having weapons. Somebody could get themself killed."

"So why you packin' it then?"

"I refuse to argue in front of a stranger. Now get your business done. You have schoolwork." With that, Puma's mother went into the kitchen, relieved that Carver wasn't a cop or a goon. She stayed in the kitchen—probably so she wouldn't hear what her son was up to.

At first Puma pleaded ignorance about the stolen Canon and Bingo's Pawnshop, but when Carver informed him of the shootout and the hot roll of film, Puma's denials faded.

"But how do I know you aren't one of the dudes gunning for me?" Puma asked.

"Quite simple. If I were, I'd have blown you to kingdom come in the hall. More to the point, how do you know somebody's gunning for you?"

"Come on, man, that's part of doin' business," Puma replied. "Somebody lookin' for you, you better know real fast. A bro' got wind of the dude in the Chevy askin' around about a Puma, and I heard right quick. I caught your whole show from the deli on the corner. How come you ain't wounded?"

"I'm a photographer, and to take pictures around here you need thick skin."

"You lost me. What are you talkin' about?"

"It's not important. The guy who was after me—what did he look like?"

"Your typical white lowlife."

"Try being a little more specific," Carver said.

"He was 'bout thirty, I'd say. Built like you, but with a beer gut. Bad dresser like you, too. Reddish hair, pockmarked face. Mean-lookin' dude."

Carver thought about the pictures he'd taken outside of Bingo's. It had to be the same guy. "Yeah, go on."

"He jumped back in the car 'bout three minutes after you took that dive into the building. Heard the cop sirens. Now I'm not hot on the bluecoats either, so I waited for the coast to clear, then came up here and bumped into your rude mug. Now, my man, I suggest you put on your shoes and socks and hit the pavement."

Only then did Carver realize he was still barefoot, but he didn't budge. "The name's Carver, and I'll leave when I'm finished.

Here's the deal. I gotta know where you stole the camera, so I can figure out what in hell is going down here."

"How much you wanna spend?" Puma asked, perking up.

"How much you wanna live? You keep stealin' people's cameras, sooner or later you'll get your butt in a wringer."

"What else am I gonna do? You think I steal cameras for sport? What you think the chances are of a three-hundred-pound black teenager getting an honest job and saving up enough money for college?"

"At this point, I'd say any job would be better than what you got—and what you got are a bunch of sleazeballs after you. They play hardball, Puma. They're not a couple of tourists from Jersey after their long-lost Instamatic. They're looking to kill us. And the sooner you catch on, the sooner I split."

"So make your pitch, man."

"You tell me where you stole the camera, and I check out the place and try to find out who we're up against."

"You got a deal. But I can't go legit without any seed money. I'll be needin' a retainer."

Chapter Sixteen

At six o'clock at the *Daily News*, Brud Siracusa left the elevator at the seventh floor. Ralph Dempsey was waiting for him in the reception area.

"Hi, Mr. Dempsey? I'm Special Agent Wilson," said Siracusa, flashing a phony I.D. "I called earlier about a photographer named Carver. Is he here yet?"

When Ralph shook his head no, Brud said he wanted to ask a few questions. Ralph consented, and led the way down the white, marble-walled corridor. He slid a plastic card through the electronic security system, opened the door, and led his visitor into the newsroom.

Ralph pointed to two empty seats by the copy desk, but Brud declined—too many reporters around, trying to file their Sunday stories and leave in time to grab dinner and a movie.

"You have somewhere private?" Brud asked.

Ralph took him to a small, glassed-in office on the Forty-first Street side of the building. Ralph sat behind the desk, and Brud took the couch. He removed his tan, kid leather gloves but left his camel hair overcoat on.

"Tell me about this guy Carver. I'll keep whatever you say in strict confidence."

Ralph leaned back in his chair and smiled. "What's Carver done this time? Must be serious for you to come in here on a Saturday. Don't tell me—he took a picture of one of your buddies being arrested for lewdness."

Brud frowned. "Spare me the humor, Mr. Dempsey," he said. "I want comedy, I go to a show. This is heavy business. A colleague died in a car crash on Thursday, and your photographer was there. He may not be implicated, but I want to talk to him, find out what he knows. Meantime, I'll need you to provide some background on him."

"You're not going to pin much on Carver, I'll tell you that," Ralph said, smile gone. "He's a straight shooter. He'll cut corners and bend rules to get his photographs, but he doesn't run people off the road."

"How long you known him?"

"I met Carver about twenty years ago. We were both on tryout at the *News*. He was a gofer in the photo department, I was a minority intern in sports. One day my boss says he needs a shot of a big prizefight out at Yankee Stadium, and he needs it in time for the two-star edition.

"I tell him it's impossible because you can't take a picture, fight traffic back to the *News*, and develop the film that fast. He says he doesn't care how I do it—work it out with Photo.

"Carver was the film runner that night. I told him the problem. Carver shrugged and left.

"About a half hour to deadline, the sports editor's getting nervous. If Carver's not back soon, there won't be time to process the film and pull a print. Fifteen minutes later, Carver saunters in and the sports editor starts to chew him out—until Carver holds up a strip of developed negatives.

"We make the deadline, and Carver's an instant hero—until he submits his expense report. A hundred bucks to rent an ambulance and driver for an hour. Turns out he developed the negs in the back while the ambulance blared its sirens and ran every red light between Yankee Stadium and here.

"That's the only kind of stuff you'll ever nail him for."

Brud looked at his watch, unimpressed. "What about ties to organized crime?"

"Believe me, there's nothing organized about Carver. All I know is he likes to hang around police stations, and he's gotten chummy with a few mobsters," Ralph said. "He tries to photograph them from flattering angles when they're arrested, gives them cigarettes in exchange for a news tip or two. That's no sin. That's the way the city works."

Brud looked at his watch again and asked where he might find Carver now.

"Depends on what's going on," Ralph said. "He's got a flat somewhere in the Village, but he lives out of his car a lot. Or he'll sleep at the Ninth Precinct station house when he thinks things are about to start hopping down there."

Brud asked specifically about the Cherokee accident. Ralph assured him that Carver was there because he seemed to have a knack for knowing when and where disaster would hit.

Brud seemed unconvinced, but he was out of questions and Carver was still a no-show. As Brud stood, Ralph Dempsey gave him a final bit of advice: "Whatever you plan to do, don't try to jack Carver around. He's the most stubborn SOB I ever met. If you bust his chops over something stupid, you can count on one thing. You'll pay."

"Is that a threat?"

"No, sir," Ralph replied. "In the newspaper business, we call that a fact."

Ralph seemed surprised, even pleased, by his bit of bravado, but that soon ended. Brud walked to the desk and rammed his left forefinger into Ralph's rib cage.

"Look, douchebag, this isn't the movies. This is serious business. You play the wise guy, you get your black ass in a sling. I call your publisher, tell him you threatened a federal officer, and you'll be hawking papers in Times Square before you know what hit you."

Ralph feigned a smile and led him to the elevators. He'd have to talk to Carver about this. Let him have it good.

Chapter Seventeen

It took maybe three minutes from the time Will Carver phoned his artist buddy, Allie, to his arrival at the gallery's back door. By then, the steeplechase was becoming routine: out the rear door to Puma's building, across a few courtyards, and over an eight-foot wall.

Allie had water boiling on the stove when he slid back the three deadbolts on the door and led Carver into the brick-walled kitchen. While Allie got him a blanket, Carver tossed two teaspoons of instant coffee into a bulky earthenware mug, then added water and a splash of condensed milk.

Carver hadn't seen Allie in six months, since the night Allie said he was quitting his job as a part-time pasteup artist at the *News* to open the gallery.

Not that Allie had a choice at that point. Allie was an ingenuous kid from Long Island. One trip to the burgeoning gallery scene in Alphabet City and he was reborn a Bohemian. No more T-shirt and jeans. He shaved his head and started wearing ripped sweatshirts and parachute pants with more pockets than a pool table—and splattered with enough paint to cover a coffeehouse.

No sooner had Allie donned the uniform of nonconformity than the *News* switched him to the late-night shift. That way the ledger pushers wouldn't see him. After selling a few paintings at a group show, Allie got a grubstake from his older brother and opened the Acme Gallery.

"Sorry I missed your first one-man show, Allie. Meant to come, but you know how it goes."

"No sweat, Carver. You wouldn't be too hot for my new stuff anyhow."

"I'll take your word for it," Carver said. "I'm not big on finger painting."

Allie responded with a cross-eyed grin. In his early twenties, Allie was still a naïf, and he never knew how to read Carver.

"Allie, I'm kidding."

"Yeah, right, gotcha," Allie replied. He returned to his Mona Lisa smile.

Carver stirred his coffee with his finger and looked around the room: Skid Row minimalist. You could take the dumpiest quarters, expose the brick or cover the walls with a fresh coat of flat white paint, and you'd pass muster in Lower Manhattan.

"Place looks good, Allie."

"I'm working on it. Not to change the subject, but you said over the phone you were in a mess. . . ."

Carver fielded the question as vaguely as he could. He admitted to taking a little heat over a stolen camera, and added he was merely trying to return it to the rightful owner before the police botched everything.

"Sure, and I'm Robert Motherwell," Allie said. "Look, give me a holler if this mess gets any messier. I know karate."

"Yeah, but these guys know machine guns. Thanks for the coffee, but I gotta get on the case again. Somebody might be back."

"Will you be warm enough?"

"Don't worry. I'm wearing bulletproof insulation."

They went to the front of the gallery, and Carver was relieved that Allie didn't turn on the lights. It wasn't that he was afraid the goon in the Nova would see him. He just didn't want to get into another discussion of modern art.

So far as Carver was concerned, the camera had put artists out of commission decades ago, and they were reduced to slopping oil on canvas and selling new clothes to the emperors uptown. In the semidarkness, Allie's paintings looked to be bad impressionistic renderings of the atomic bomb plumes at Hiroshima and Nagasaki. The nicest thing Carver could say about them was that he liked the frames.

Fortunately, the two men stood in silence and waited for the Nova to drive by. Carver soon grew anxious. The flak jacket felt as heavy as an iron lung long about now, and his T-shirt was soaked with sweat.

The vigil took five minutes. When the Nova drove past, Carver slipped out the door and tried to catch the license plate before the Nova turned north. He raced after it, and felt his right knee click with every stride. By the time he reached the corner, the Nova had vanished.

He didn't see it again until he rounded the corner onto Fifth Street and spotted it in front of Puma's building. The motor was running. In the darkness, Carver slipped into a doorway to scout the situation. The rain began to pick up again, and it was tough to see what was happening ahead.

In the excitement, Carver had forgotten the bullet meant for his back. Now, in the bitter-cold downpour, his shoulder blade felt like somebody'd bushwhacked him with a ballpeen hammer.

This guy wanted to play rough? Carver decided to return the heat. He clung close to the buildings as he made his approach. In a minute's time, he crept his way to the car's rear bumper. Rain dripped from the brim of the Phillies cap as he took out the wire and adjusted the loop to a foot in diameter.

He finished just in time. The rain eased, and the thug got out of his car and walked to Puma's building. As he reached out to press the door buzzer, Carver moved in from behind, looping the wire lasso around the thug's neck before the guy could react.

Both hands on the wire, Carver dropped to the ground, letting the weight of his body draw the makeshift noose taut. The force snapped the thug to his knees—like a sailfish who'd had a hook set in his jaw.

The Phillies cap flew off in the commotion. A hand groped for Carver's hair and nearly ripped it from his scalp. The pain made him yank harder.

The thug lost the tug-of-war when his body started to convulse. Carver struggled to keep his balance in the doorway, then managed to plant his left foot on the man's back. At that point, Carver pulled for all he was worth.

"Give up?"

When the thug's body went slack, Carver stood and yanked his quarry against the building's metal door.

"Hands up, then spread 'em," Carver ordered, taking a line from an old TV show. The man obeyed, and Carver reached around to extract a pistol from the man's shoulder holster and a wallet from his pants pocket.

"You a cop?"

"How'd you guess?"

"I want my lawyer."

"You have the right to shut the hell up. Now we walk to the car, real slow. That's it." As a reminder, Carver gave the improvised choke collar another pull, then bent down and retrieved his Phillies cap. "Unlock the passenger door and slide across."

When Carver climbed in alongside, the thug finally got a good look at Carver's face. "You're the frickin' photographer."

"That's right. Now start the car and get us out of here." As the Nova pulled away from the curb, Carver got down to business.

"Time you and me had ourselves a talk."

"I ain't tellin' you nothin'."

Carver gave the wire a yank. "That's the trouble with creeps like you. You're good at shooting people in the back, but otherwise you tend to choke. Now I want you to tell me what's going on. Who's on that roll of film?"

Silence.

Carver gave the wire another yank. "Does 'queens' or 'ace' mean anything to you?"

"Yeah. Queens is where my mother lives. Ace is the name of my comb."

Carver tried Plan B. "Okay, have it your way. Here's the story. Drive down to East Third Street between First and Second. There'll be a funeral parlor in the middle of the second block. I'll leave you there with a message for whoever you're working for. Make sure he gets it."

When the Nova swung onto Third Street, Carver finished his instructions. "The funeral home'll be up ahead on the right. Park in the No Standing zone. After I leave, go tell your boss that it's over. History. I would have given you the film, just to have you scumdogs off my back. But you trashed my apartment, you killed

THE LAST FRAME 69

my friend, and I'm plum out of patience. Now you can forget your photos. Forget Puma. Forget me. So go take some other porno shots and leave me alone, got that?"

The thug sneered. "I'll pass along what you said, but you're wasting your breath. We'll get the photos back one way or another."

"Maybe I'll just burn 'em."

"And then maybe we'll just have to kill you. I was only trying to get your attention when I shot at you earlier. Unfortunately for you, my aim was a little low."

"Well, you have my attention now, and you're going to pay."

The thug parked the Nova in front of the funeral home. Carver ordered him to place his hands behind his head, then Carver wrapped the wire taut against the man's wrists and secured it to the headrest. With the thug immobilized, Carver removed the man's wallet, read the name on the driver's license, then placed the billfold and the pistol on the floor.

"Don't push me any further . . . Mo." Carver squinted to read the license by the light of the dashboard. "Don't push me any further, Mo Orsinski, or you'll be joining Bingo in the land down under."

After making sure the street was empty, Carver walked around to the driver's side of the car. Using a car key, he scratched a message on the door, then disappeared into the night.

Chapter Eighteen

The Sunday *Daily News* sells more than one million, six hundred thousand copies—more than any other newspaper in the United States. The presses roll from six P.M. Saturday till dawn, consuming five hundred tons of newsprint in the process.

To keep as timely as possible, the paper replates a handful of pages of news and sports several times during the night. Reporters, editors, photographers, layout artists, and pressmen battle deadlines in cycles a few hours apart, fueled by deli coffee, antacid tablets, and a dose of anxiety. If a major story breaks at nine P.M. and doesn't make part of the press run, there'll be hell to pay come Monday morning.

When Will Carver phoned Ralph Dempsey at eight P.M. and said he had a Page One photo possibility, the line went silent as Dempsey worked out a mental timetable: maybe a half hour to get a photographer to take the photo and get it back to the *News*, eight minutes to run the film through one of the three automated processors, another ten to pull a good print. Then it'd have to run through the copy desk for a cutline, and on to engraving . . .

When Dempsey finished the arithmetic, he replied: "It's a possibility. Now, what you got for me?"

"Another good crime shot. Two-bit hood with a wire noose strapping him to the front seat of a stolen car. Still alive—looks like some sort of mob warning. In case anybody asks, you didn't hear this from me."

Carver gave Ralph the address, then added: "Now do me a favor. If you have a reporter you can spare at this hour, send him down to the Ninth Precinct station house. When the cops haul this

this thug in, have the reporter find out what the guy's story is, and look to see what number he dials if he makes any calls.

"I don't have much more to give you now. It's only a hunch—but I think this is tied to Bingo's murder. The reporter won't get much into tomorrow's paper, but it could lead to a big story in a day or two."

Ralph agreed, then added: "Meanwhile, your bogus FBI agent dropped by earlier. We can talk about it Monday, but you owe me, Carver. You owe me."

Mo Orsinski sat stewing in the back of the blue-and-white. He was pissed at himself—never should have shot at the dirtbag photographer, never should have gone back looking for the kid. But Brud had sounded so nasty about it, Mo didn't dare come back empty-handed.

While the cops finished their work outside, Mo tried to concoct an explanation that would get him off the hook with the cops—one that would satisfy Brud later on. It had been humiliating enough to get ambushed and tied up in a stolen car, but then some photographer arrived to take his picture and called the police.

Still, what could the cops nail him on? They couldn't prove that he stole the car. They couldn't trace the gun to him. Simple: He'd just say as little as possible and stick to his story—he'd been jumped by some weirdo (which, he was convinced, was true) and left for dead inside somebody's Nova.

The cops would run a check on him, see the assault charges on his rap sheet, and try to hold him overnight, but they had nothing on him this time. He'd call Brud from the police station, have him send a lawyer. And Mo'd be sprung in time to catch the eleven o'clock news.

A patrolman walked over and shined his flashlight on the Nova's front door, then trained it on Mo's face. "Got another question for you, dog breath. There's a message scrawled on the front door here. Perhaps you'd like to explain it to me. It says, 'I killed Bingo.'"

Will Carver was almost to Gina's apartment building before the weight of what he'd done began to register. He'd almost killed a man, but he'd had no choice. It was war, and Carver didn't know how big an army he was up against.

Now he worried for Gina. If the other side ever connected her with him, they'd kill her. He had to find out who was behind all of this and cut a deal quick. . . .

Puma's story had been about what he'd expected. One night last week Puma had been in the West Village, looking to roll a homosexual or two. He saw a Benz outside a brownstone on Jane Street and waited to see if he could mug the owner.

Next thing Puma knew, a blond-haired guy left a house two doors down, carrying a tripod and a vinyl camera bag. Puma walked up behind him, jammed a finger in the guy's back, and told him to drop the bag or kiss his sweet ass good-bye.

When the guy obliged, Puma gave him a kidney punch, grabbed the bag, and shoved him into a trash can. He ran three blocks, grabbed the Canon and two lenses, ditched the bag, and took a cab across town. Sold the camera equipment to Bingo the next day.

And like any smart entrepreneur with repeat business in mind, Puma had memorized the address.

No point checking out the place now. Carver could run a check on it tomorrow. He stopped at a liquor store and bought four dollars' worth of wine. He was at Gina's by eight-thirty.

Gina came to the door in a housecoat. Her hair was up, and her face was clean of makeup. She seemed relieved to see him.

"How'd it go?"

"Not bad, but I'm beat," he said. He took off his peacoat and flak jacket. "All I want to do is get warm, get dry, and drink my wine. I don't feel like talking."

Gina insisted.

Reluctantly, he told her of his first encounter with the goon and the meeting with Puma, but chose not to mention the garroting. His mistake. He did remember to thank her for stopping by the precinct house for the flak jacket.

"Actually," he added, "I ought to wear it all the time, considering the scrapes I manage to get myself into."

He twisted the cap off the wine. "Want a swig?"

"No, thanks. I think I'll stick to Tab. But I'll get you a glass—and a blanket."

She walked to a cupboard and called to him: "One last question, and I'll let you be. I see the pictures you take, I hear about these exploits, and I keep wondering how the hell you fell into this smarmy line of work."

"Just lucky, I guess."

"How about giving me a straight answer for once?"

"I got the wine if you got the time."

Carver explained that he'd come to Manhattan in the early seventies in search of a job, answered a classified ad for a gofer at the *Daily News*, and gradually worked his way up to photo lab assistant. One Monday, on his day off, he was cooking breakfast and listening to the radio when he heard about a big mob hit in a swank Midtown hotel.

According to the newscaster, the head of a local crime family had been executed, and the entire hotel had been cordonned off while Forensics performed all of its invariably worthless procedures—dusting for nonexistent fingerprints, calculating the trajectory of the bullets, estimating how long the stiff had been that way.

Nothing better to do, Carver packed his gear and took the RR up to Sixtieth Street and Fifth Avenue. When he reached the lobby of the hotel, however, he couldn't get through the police check. He saw a *News* photographer there, in the process of trying to bribe a cop to take him up to the penthouse and let him get the shot he needed.

This time the cops were playing it straight. In New York, when a mob chieftain dies, you'd think it were the Pope.

Then the *News* photographer spied Carver, walked over, and remarked: "Hey, what you doing here, trying to cut my grass? Don't waste your time. Nobody's getting a shot of that stiff except the police photographer. We'll have to get to him later."

Carver followed the photographer outside, and that's when he got his brainstorm. He looked up at the penthouse and tried to figure a way to get up there. Then he noticed the window washer on a scaffold two buildings over.

A half hour and an empty wallet later, the new window washer walked through the lobby, brushed past the police, and took the elevator to the top floor. He looked around and saw the elevator to the penthouse. It required a room key to operate, so he lugged his window-washing gear, a rope, and a bucket up two flights of stairs to the roof. He peered over the edge of the roof. The balcony loomed twelve feet below.

The rope took care of that. He lowered himself to the corner of the patio, behind a big potted evergreen. He peered through a window into the master bedroom. One glance told him why the cops were so nervous.

Sitting upright on the bed, deader than Dillinger and nakeder than a pigeon's butt, were the gangster and two young women. The wall behind them was splattered worse than a Jackson Pollock canvas.

Carver quietly took his Speed Graphic from the bucket and hooked up the flash while the Forensics boys finished their talcum powder routine. When they took a break, he slipped through the sliding glass doors.

Once in the master bedroom, he discreetly pulled the sheets up and over the naked chests—the *News* being a family newspaper—and took a nice group portrait.

He was out the door and halfway across the balcony when the elevator door opened. Carver had no other choice. He hastily flung the camera onto the roof and calmly began washing the windows.

The cops were not pleased. "Yo! What the hell you think you're doin'?"

The next Carver knew, one cop had him by the collar and the other was frisking him. They asked him for his I.D., and he reached inside his white jumpsuit and produced his wallet and driver's license.

"Well, Mr. Carver, take it from me. Forget what you saw or your days as a window washer are over."

The cops proceeded to escort their window washer and his gear to the elevator and told him to beat it. He went down one flight, then walked up to the roof and retrieved his camera.

When he reached the News Building, he went straight to the darkroom. He emerged with a five-thousand-dollar shot.

That night he was on his second bottle of Möet when he got the call. It was a young assistant news editor named Ralph Dempsey.

"Hey, Carver, just called to tell you what a great shot you took today. But you already know that. Only one problem on this end. Union rules say a darkroom assistant can't take photos for this paper. So what I'm trying to say here is that as of yesterday, you're fired. Come on in tomorrow and we'll see about getting you a new job."

Maybe it was the champagne, maybe it was sudden confidence, but that night he fell asleep thinking about his newfound fame. He'd become a staff photographer for sure. Maybe he'd win a Pulitzer.

When Carver arrived in the newsroom the next morning, the managing editor waved him over to his office. "Carver, got a minute? We have a problem here. I know you did a great job for us, but we have to let you go.

"I know it sounds crazy, but half of Manhattan wants your hindquarters handed to you. The union's steamed because you were cutting in on their turf. The cops are steamed, officially because you broke the law and unofficially because you made them look bad. And the mob is steamed because they don't like their bloody laundry hanging out to dry on Page One.

"So here's the offer. You can't work here anymore, but I'll still buy your stuff—free-lance. If you don't make a big deal out of it and the union cools off, I'll even give you free run of the darkroom. Agreed?"

Carver nodded yes.

"That's it for now," the managing editor said as he gestured toward the door. "I wouldn't hang around here today. I forgot to tell you who else is steamed. The mayor. One of the bimbos in the photograph was his niece."

Chapter Nineteen

SUNDAY MORNING

At ten A.M., Brud Siracusa locked his office and decided it was time to go for a run. He had planned to get caught up on some paperwork first, but the phone kept ringing. First it was some tenants with a leaky toilet on Houston Street. Brud told them to go to their super. Then it was a tenant with no hot water. Brud told him to go to his super. Then Tracey called. Brud's impulse was to tell his partner where to go, but he thought better of it. Didn't anybody go to church anymore?

As Brud descended the stairs, Tracey's words still rang in his ear: "What are you twits doing over there? You guys are supposed to be helping me blackmail somebody and you end up on the front page of the *Daily News*. You're making me frightfully nervous."

Brud had tried to convince him that some junkie had mugged Mo and left him for dead, but his partner wasn't buying. "That's malarkey. What's going on?"

Brud assured him that everything was under control, told him he'd explain everything later, then hung up. And left the phone off the hook. Brud returned to the ledger sheets, but he couldn't concentrate. What if his partner stopped by and started pressing him? Or worse, what if his partner started pressing Mo for information? It had taken Brud ten minutes to worm everything out of Mo—how long would it take his partner?

He needed a run. Yesterday's storm front had finally moved

on, and the sun felt soothing as he jogged past the playground on Sixth Avenue. The temperature was fifty degrees, and Brud sensed this would be the last nice day before winter took up permanent residence.

When he reached the basketball courts, Brud began to psych himself. Crunch time was near. He stopped for a moment to watch a Sunday pick-up game and remembered his old playing days, the days when he was in high school and in the big time, the days before CCNY and the stinking match courses and the expulsion for sucker punching a tweedy prof who had called Brud to the front of the class and accused him of cheating. Even the coach couldn't bail him out of that one. No more scholarship, no more basketball, no more limelight.

That was the year that his uncle got him a job working for a mob-connected construction outfit, and Brud discovered he wasn't cut out for honest work. So he went back to his uncle, hat in hand, and asked to be set up in another line of work.

His uncle asked what he was good at, aside from basketball. Brud mentioned his boxing, and how he'd used it from time to time to collect money for a few campus dope dealers. His uncle said that getting involved with drug dealers was strictly for losers. But he added that he wouldn't mind seeing how persuasive Brud was, and gave him a few collection jobs. Brud got past-due rent money from three tenants and hospitalized the fourth with a broken jaw. His uncle eventually set Brud up in his current job, managing a dozen run-down apartment buildings south of Fourteenth Street.

Brud got a hundred dollars a week salary, plus ten percent of all the past-due rents he collected. Few tenants paid on time, and he also made good money on the side by threatening to tell Immigration on them. In all, he made a decent buck, but his life had played like a stuck phonograph record ever since.

Now high school, that had been different. Brud was point guard on a team with two all-city players, and they had waltzed their way to the championship game a decade earlier.

The game was held at the Garden on a Saturday afternoon, and his team played unconscious. Brud ran the fast break, and his pals dunked everything but the doughnuts on the press table.

With five minutes left, Brud's team led by a dozen and started thinking about the postgame celebration—slapping low fives during time-outs and getting fancy with their upcourt passes. The other team put on a full-court press, and before Brud and his teammates knew it, the clock was down to two minutes and their lead had dropped to four. The coach started to scream at his players from the bench, and his panic rubbed off.

The star forward launched a brick, the other team got the rebound, and the lead was soon down to two. After another bad miss, a fast break tied the score.

Brud dribbled the ball to mid-court and motioned for a time-out. For once, the coach regained his composure. He told the team to play loose, work the clock down to ten seconds, and play for the last shot: "With five ticks left, get the ball to Siracusa and clear out the lane. His man's been playing off him too far all afternoon.

"And, Brud, one more thing. You don't have the greatest range, so don't try any bombs. You drive on this guy, you'll catch him flat-footed and have an easy lay-up. If the center comes over to help out, dish the ball to Williams underneath."

As Brud returned to the floor, his hands felt numb and his stomach churned. People called it choking, but it came from deep down in the gut, and Brud had that feeling.

He caught the inbounds pass and flipped it to Williams, Mr. All-City. Maybe Williams wouldn't be able to get the ball back to him. Maybe Williams would be forced to shoot it himself. Brud was looking for a way to dodge the bullet, but as the clock reached eight seconds, instinct took over.

Brud slid over to take a bounce pass at the top of the key and started down the lane, in command. Sure enough, his defender stuttered for half a second as Brud feinted left and went by him. Then he squared up and took a ten-foot jumper. . . .

Brud smiled at the memory now, pictured himself gliding into the air, releasing the ball crisply with his left hand, watching it reach the top of its arc and float silently through the hoop.

That was the secret then, and that was the secret now. Carver was playing too far off him. Time to feel Carver out. And when the time came, drive on him and shoot. Maybe tonight he'd meet Carver, end his little game.

Brud awoke from his thoughts at the sound of an errant pass bounding in his direction. Brud went through the chain link gate, retrieved the basketball, and motioned that he wanted to take a shot. The teenagers smirked at him. But when he started to dribble toward the basket, a wiry black kid came up to guard him.

Switching his dribble to his right hand, Brud worked his way to the top of the key. The other players hooted at Brud to shoot, but he bided his time. As he neared the foul line, he pulled up and threw a head fake. His defender jumped to block the shot, and Brud faded left, putting an extra snap in his wrist as he released the ball.

Swish.

He didn't wait for their reaction. He simply strode off the court, thinking: Nobody messes with Brud Siracusa and wins. Not when the game is on the line.

Chapter Twenty

Will Carver was knee-deep in a nightmare about a tenement fire when Gina Constantine awoke him, and he was too dazed to respond.

He had dreamed he had responded to a two-alarm fire that he'd heard about on his police radio. As he arrived on the scene, smoke billowed from an open third-floor window. A young girl in pigtails and pajamas was screaming for help from the fire escape. He wanted to rescue her, but he couldn't move. All he could do was look up at her and take her picture, until she was consumed by the smoke.

"You were screaming, Will." Gina hovered over him, arms around a copy of the Sunday *News*.

"Tell me something I don't know," he mumbled. He rubbed the stubble on his face and started to recall the night before, especially the wine.

"You're in a foul mood."

"It was a foul dream." The nightmare had been so vivid that Carver's throat felt parched from the smoke. "What time is it?"

"Time to talk." She plopped the heavy tabloid onto his lap. "Why did you lie to me last night?"

"I don't know what you're talking about. You just woke me up from a horrendous dream. Gimme a minute to think straight."

"Maybe this'll help," Gina said, and pointed to the front page. "I thought I'd go out for coffee and bagels while you slept. Then I walk past the corner newsstand and see this—a photo of some guy nearly strangled with a wire outside a funeral parlor on East Third. Try to tell me you weren't involved."

The Last Frame

"Give me another minute. I'll take a shower and get dressed while you cool off."

"Better come up with a good story, Will. From the looks of this photograph, we're talking aggravated assault. As far as I can see, I'm harboring a criminal. I work for the police, remember? I want you out of this apartment now."

He looked up at Gina and lost his train of thought. Perhaps it was purely collision avoidance, but he was struck by how good she looked in the morning light. No makeup again, a soft white wool turtleneck, gold hoop earrings, her long black hair pulled back. He had always figured that most women without makeup were like barrooms—you were really better off if you didn't see how they looked in broad daylight. Another myth destroyed.

"You know," he said, stifling a yawn, "you really look pretty decent without makeup."

Gina bit a fingernail. "What are you, nuts? Aren't you listening to what I'm telling you?"

"What am I supposed to say?" he replied. "Okay, I lied. I'm sorry. The last thing I want to do is argue with you, but these guys aren't playing dodgeball. The thug on the front page shot me in the back, and no doubt killed Bingo."

He stood and tried to point to a black-and-blue mark the size of a silver dollar: "You think I was going to let him walk? How else do you fight fire?"

"This isn't Dodge City. You could've called the police."

"And they'd ask me why I was wearing a bulletproof vest, what I was doing over there in Alphabet City, who was after me, and why. Then they'd type a report and that'd be the end of it—and I'd still have some thugs trying to kill me. Now maybe the idiots will back off. Excuse me. I gotta wash up."

Under the jet of hot water in the shower, Carver felt a jackhammer headache coming on. He'd been in jams before, but nothing the likes of this. He'd driven one guy off the road. Another—Mo—had murdered Bingo. Carver had dirty pictures he didn't want, yet people were shooting at him to get them back. This couldn't be plain old vanilla blackmail. It had to involve somebody wealthy, somebody famous, somebody important. Somebody sick.

He went over the words of the dying man in the Jeep, but nothing added up. What did queens and aces have to do with it?

The shower lifted his spirits, and he used Gina's pink disposable razor to shave. It was dull, and he had to scrape the bristles from his face. Outside the bathroom door sat his clothes neatly washed and folded. He stepped into his jeans, put on the white shirt, and walked into the living room. His knee started to click again, but it was the least of his worries.

Gina sat on the couch. Her shoulders were stooped. She was taking a drag off a cigarette and staring vacantly at the carpet.

"I didn't know you smoked," Carver said.

"Only in emergencies." Gina looked at him and gave him an icy glare. "You're turning me into a wreck. Don't you give a damn about anybody else? You'd be out the door already if it weren't for that nasty welt on your back. I believe that somebody took a shot at you last night, but trying to strangle the guy? That's out of control."

Carver sat beside her on the couch and rubbed his scalp. It ached from that thug, Mo, trying to rip out his hair.

He was losing his patience. "I didn't try to kill anybody. I was only making a point. I said I didn't want to get you in the middle of this. And you aren't—not yet. Nobody knows where I am, and nobody's going to finger me for mugging a sleazeball."

The cigarette sizzled as she doused it in her coffee cup. "I'm listening."

"I can split now and you'll never see me again. I'll leave town, move to East Bejeezus, if that's what you want. I've tried not to get you sucked into this mess, but it's like dog crap. Once you step in it, you can never completely scrape it off. These guys won't quit, so neither can I. At this point, they've turned me into one ornery bastard, and I want to see this through. You can hate me—or help. At this point, I don't care anymore."

"You can stay a while longer," Gina said.

He sensed that her heart wasn't it. "I wouldn't want you to go out on a limb for me."

Gina didn't reply for several moments. Her instincts told her not to get involved, but deep down she sensed she needed to. Ever since her husband's death, she'd been cut off from this sort of excitement. At the station house, she didn't feel like part of the team anymore—just another dispatcher. At least now she was in the thick of things again.

"What do you want me to do?" she said, and gently placed her hand on his knee.

"Just go about your normal routine," he said. "You work tonight?"

"No, they do give me weekends off sometimes. In fact, I was just thinking that maybe you'd like to pay some room and board by taking me to dinner tonight."

"So long as it's fairly cheap. It's not that I don't appreciate your help. It's just that I'm low on dough right now. I don't know what I'd do without you."

"You'd get yourself killed, but you'll probably do that anyway." Gina wasn't smiling when she said it.

"Well, if I'm not in your way, I'd just like to hang out a while, have a cup of coffee, read the paper, just get my mind straight. I gotta run an errand this afternoon. I need to pick up that money the *News* owes me and do a little research on the side."

He looked at the front page of the Sunday *News*. There, staring at him, was Mo's scowling mug. Crap, they'd cropped out the message he had scratched into the Nova's front door. Then he saw the credit line—Karen Connell, one of the photography department's concessions to equal opportunity. She was in her late twenties, a go-getter who'd put him out of business before long if she kept hustling after pictures. He began to fume. He did all the work, and she snapped the picture and got the credit.

His mood didn't improve when Gina remembered to tell him she'd located his car: "It wasn't stolen after all. The police towed it. It's over in the pound on the West Side. It'll take two hundred bucks to get it out when the towing garage opens tomorrow—one hundred fifty for the tow, thirty-five for the ticket, and another fifteen for storage."

Carver grunted, but Gina wouldn't let it pass. "Come off it. You should be happy. Your car's okay."

"Right. And where am I supposed to get that kind of money? Damned cops . . . Sorry. I forgot I was talking to one. But it occurs to me that while Bingo was getting shot to death, your pals were busy towing my Rabbit. . . . Wait a minute. I have NYP plates. Cops don't tow cars with NYP plates."

"They do whenever one of the local papers does a series on police corruption, which the *Times* did last week, remember? It's just the department's way of saying thanks for the free publicity."

"Swell. Now what do I do?"

"I can lend you some money," Gina said.

"No way. Borrowing money is the quickest way to wreck a friendship."

"Who said we were friends?"

Chapter Twenty-one

The message from Tracey awaited on the answering machine when Brud Siracusa got home after his run:
"Brud, it's ten past noon. I'm calling because I'm tired of your runaround. Discussing our mutual problem over the phone is obviously useless, especially when you insist on hanging up on me. You seem to forget we're on the same side. We need to get together and work out a mutually satisfactory strategy. We can't drag this crap out any longer, if you'll pardon the expression. We have to put the plan in motion, film or no film. I'll be at the Cedar Tavern at four P.M. I expect to see you then. And do us both a favor. Leave Brother Mo out of this."

Brud checked the clock above the breakfast table. Two P.M. Plenty of time to shower, get a bite to eat, get organized. The sitdown with Tracey probably wasn't such a bad idea anyway. Tracey had sounded like he had a plan, and at this stage of the game Brud was willing to try anything that would get him his sorely needed money as soon as possible.

The thought of money reminded Brud of Mo—Mo was supposed to be out making a few collections. Sundays were the best day for that type of work, since you had a good chance of finding the chumps at home. And that might mean some spending money. No sense in suffering while he waited for the big cash to come in.

Brud pecked out Mo's number on the push-button phone. Mo answered on the third ring. "Hey, Mo. Just thought I'd give you a quick buzz to remind you that today's collection day. . . . No, not at all. I knew you wouldn't forget, but I just wanted to make sure you weren't worrying about Carver and that stupid message he scrawled on the car door last night. You did fine. In fact, I got to thinking about it last night, and you did more than fine. We finally made contact with the dirtbag, and we know he still has our film. Not only that, you gotta believe he's going to come to us with it, just to get us off his back. He has nothing to gain by hanging on to it, and everything to lose. Am I right? You bet I am. . . ."

Mo said he wanted to go after the Puma when he was done with his collection run, but Brud wasn't keen on it. "No, let's forget about Puma for the day. He has to be dealt with, but he's not a key player. You're too wound up. Use your energy—go bust some renters' heads and get us some folding money to line our pockets.

"By the way, you don't know how Syracuse did against West Virginia, do you? They won?" Brud smacked his hand against a kitchen cabinet. "Dammit. I tried to lay some money on the 'Cuse yesterday, but couldn't get a bookie to take my money. . . . Yes, Mo, I know my credit's crap. But we'll change that soon enough, right? I'll let you get about your business. Talk to you tonight, after eight."

Brud put the phone receiver down. Just takin' care of business, Brud said to himself. Just takin' care of business. Now it was time to shower and get ready for the other business at hand, old tricky Tracey.

On his way to the bathroom, he stripped off his sweat gear and tossed it into the hamper. He grabbed the blue terry cloth towel that hung from the bathroom door and dried his hair, then pushed his hair straight back, the way that Pat Riley, the coach of the L.A. Lakers, wore his hair on TV. Look sharp, feel sharp.

Brud paused at the full-length mirror in the hall and took full measure of himself. The razor wound was healing nicely, and the rest of him appeared as trim and muscular as ever. "If you have your health," his mother used to say, "you have everything."

Not yet I don't, Brud thought. But I will soon enough.

Tracey was standing at the bar when Brud walked in at a quarter to four. An old Lou Reed song, "Take a Walk on the Wild Side," played on the jukebox, but Brud could barely make it out over the shouting. Brud turned and looked up to see a TV above the door. It was tuned to a Giants game, and the team in blue was on its opponent's five-yard line.

"I'm glad you're early," Tracey said with a grin. "There's nothing worse than pro football. Can I get you anything? It's on the house. Professional courtesy, you know."

"A light beer would do fine," Brud told the bartender. Then to Tracey: "Where can we talk in private?"

Tracey pointed to a booth in the back. "No one will hear us back there. The Giants game has ten minutes left, and they're trailing by two, not that I give a rat's patoot. But nobody's going to pay any attention to us while the game's on."

Brud took his bottle of beer and followed Tracey toward the back. His eyes adjusted to the lighting, and he looked at the old prints and Broadway posters lining the walls as he walked. A step ahead of him, Tracey was decked out in full regalia as usual. Paisley silk shirt and purple velveteen trousers. His reddish blond hair was in a wild bouffant, and it made Brud wonder how he'd ever gotten hooked up with a flake like Tracey. Money, Brud knew. Money was the fuel that drove him to almost anything.

The two men sat across from each other, an amber restaurant candle flickering between them. Tracey spoke first. "I want you to tell me everything, love. And I mean everything. If I don't know the full score, I'll be operating on false assumptions, and that can prove fatal to both of us."

Brud started with the mugging and the stolen camera, which had occurred just after he had taken the pictures and left Tracey and the mark at the place on Jane Street. Brud said that he'd traced the camera to a pawnshop on the Bowery and learned that a newspaper photographer had bought the camera with the film still inside. . . .

Tracey jerked his head. "What's the photographer's name?"

"Carver."

Tracey winced.

"Why, you know him?"

"I've met him a few times. A bit of a lowlife if you ask me, but he's a tough nut to crack."

"That's not exactly a news bulletin, Tracey. Anyway, we've been trying to get the film back ever since, and all that Carver does is bust our chops."

"Like the photo in the *News* today?"

Brud nodded.

"Anything else I ought to know about that?"

"I think I need another beer," Brud replied, and held up his empty bottle to get the waitress's eye.

"I asked you a question, love. You said you'd come clean. What else?"

"You know the car where the cops found Mo? On the door on the driver's side, Carver had scratched a message—'I killed Bingo.' That caught the cops' attention. Apparently they're hot to catch the perpetrator."

"What did Mo tell them?"

"Not much. He asked for his lawyer. He did say that the guy who tied him up must have done it, must have left it as a confession or a taunt." Brud stopped to take a sip from the bottle.

"And they bought it?"

"Hey, I thought that was pretty good for Mo. Besides, the cops asked him where he was Friday morning when the pawnbroker was shot, and Mo said he was working at the office with me. A detective called last night around ten to follow up, and I confirmed the alibi."

"Swell, so now they got Mo's name *and* yours."

"Forget about it. The cops have zero. Squat. Nada. Nobody saw the shooting, and I had Mo toss the gun Friday afternoon. They're pissing into the wind, if they're pissing at all. The cops didn't even have enough to charge Mo with anything and keep him overnight."

"What did Mo tell the lawyer?"

"Nothing. The same story he told the cops. . . . Now, the only question is, where do we go from here?"

"I think you ought to call the mark at his home tonight and get the ball rolling. Refresh his memory about Tuesday night, and tell him you have some wonderful photos of the occasion for him to remember us by. What figure did we agree on?"

"Two hundred and fifty thousand dollars. You said that's about as much as the guy can come up with."

Tracey opened a compact and looked at his eyebrows, and Brud noticed for the first time that Tracey had filled them in with some sort of makeup. Brud looked down at his bottle of beer and peeled the label to keep from staring.

"How about Carver?" Tracey continued. "What do we do about him?"

"Well, at least Mo found out that Carver still has the pictures. Carver even told Mo that he had been willing to give 'em back to us—just to be done with the whole mess. Now I'm not so sure. Maybe we should talk money to him, cut him in on the payoff."

"Skip it. It would never work. From what I've seen of him, he's one self-righteous jerk. No, you have to appeal to his good sense—that his health may begin to fail if he doesn't come across with the film. He knows that. He'll come around. Otherwise he would have destroyed the photos already."

Brud sighed with relief.

But Tracey reapplied the pressure. "You haven't told me everything, have you? Something else is eating you, if you'll pardon the expression."

Brud took a gulp of beer. "To be completely honest, I got cash-flow problems. If I don't come up with some major cash quick, some loan shark's going to make my blood flow."

Tracey laughed. "Well put. But I don't see it as a problem. When you call the mark tonight, make him come up with the money by seven o'clock Tuesday. Tell him to drop it off at the bar after work. He won't go to the cops about this. He can't afford to. In the meantime, Carver's got to come to see things our way. He doesn't have much choice."

With that, Tracey got up, flipped a five-dollar bill on the table, and headed toward the door. As he donned his cape, he saw Brud pocket the five dollars.

Chapter Twenty-two

The reverse directory for Manhattan weighs more than five pounds. It's nearly three times as thick as a normal phone book, and it works backward. Instead of looking up a name, you find an address and get a name and phone number, or you find a phone number and get a name and address.

Most people never have any use for a reverse directory. It's intended for society's undesirables—salesmen, crooks, cops, and reporters.

Ever get a phone call in the final minute of a close football game—some jerk trying to sell life insurance or a lifetime subscription to some ludicrous publication? He probably got your name from a reverse directory.

Or take a burglar. If he's aspiring to rob a place, he looks up the address in the reverse directory, gets the phone number, then calls to see if anybody's home. No answer, he pulls up the van.

Cops use the directory in a siege situation. If they've got a loony bin candidate holed up with a hostage in some tenement, they'll look up the number and call him. Some places in Bed-Stuy don't have running water or heat, but you can count on the occupants having two things—a color TV and a telephone. And when a phone rings and somebody's home, you can bet the rent check he'll answer.

While the cops are dialing the squirrel bait, chances are reporters are thumbing through the reverse directory, too. They're looking up the address and getting the phone numbers of the neighbors to get some lively quotes. The neighbors' comments fall into two categories: "The guy's the nicest man in the building, wonderful with kids" or "he always kept to himself, but I saw him kick a dog once."

It doesn't matter who the reporter asks about. Neighbors always give one of those two replies and newspapers dutifully disseminate them to a waiting public.

Despite some bad memories, Will Carver still carried a reverse directory in his car for occasions such as this, but little good it did now, locked up on some police pier on the West Side.

The *Daily News* had a reverse directory in its library. That's where he was headed—he'd see if Ralph had found out what number Mo had called from the police station the night before, so he could trace its owner in the reverse directory. And he wanted to look up that Jane Street address to see who lived in the building where Puma had stolen the camera. With any luck, some money might await him at the *News*, too.

When Carver assumed that the *Daily News* was the last place anybody would look for him, he broke one of the three cardinal rules of newspaperdom.

One: Never believe an editor.

Two: Never betray a source.

Three: Never assume anything.

As soon as he entered the building, he knew he'd pay for his assumption. Ordinarily, the lobby of the News Building was good for a few grins. It features as its centerpiece an enormous rotating globe—big enough to give Atlas a hernia. The globe is twelve feet in diameter, and the way spotlights illuminate it, you'd think Michelangelo had made it between ceiling jobs.

On the wall nearby hang blowups of famous front pages from the *News*, the usual man-walks-on-the-moon stuff. The other self-important gimmick is a bank of clocks displaying the time in other parts of the world—just in case you thought the *News* was some small-town rag or you wanted to know the time in Tokyo or Paris.

Next to the clocks are a half dozen weather gauges giving the temperature, wind speed, barometric pressure, and so forth. Carver always assumed they were for local weather only. If you wanted to know which way the wind was blowing at the Kremlin, you were out of luck.

But his favorite attractions were the wall maps on the left—

maps of the United States, the world, and (for the very, very lost) the solar system.

He hadn't reached the map of the world when he sensed trouble. His peripheral vision had picked up a figure off to the right. Instinct. Someone standing strangely. Someone who didn't belong.

It was a man in his late forties. He wore a maroon stadium coat, wool slacks, and a Tyrolean hat with one of those silly pheasant feathers on it. He looked harmless, but Carver couldn't take any chances.

He also knew it was too late to run. If this guy was out to get him, then the only hope was to be aggressive.

Before the man could make a move, Carver wheeled and strode toward him, fists clenched for effect. "Looking for me, bub?"

Startled, the man took a step backward and bumped against the wall. The look in his eyes was unmistakable. The guy was no hoodlum. He was a zealot, and that made him twice as dangerous.

"You Carver?" the man asked, fumbling to regain his composure.

Carver tried nonchalance. "Yeah. What can I do you for?"

"I got something to say to you, hotshot," the man said. "But not here. Where can we talk?"

"There's an Automat on the corner. Will that do?"

The man agreed and followed in silence as Carver walked through the revolving brass door, down the sidewalk on Forty-second Street, and into Horn and Hardart's. The place had been renovated a couple of times in the past decade. It had art deco lettering in the window, tasteful little blinking white lights inside, and even rented itself out for parties at night nowadays, but the food still tasted the same.

The two men sat across from one another at a table near the dessert machines. The man took off his hat, placed it on the seat next to him, and began to speak. Carver interrupted: "Look, before we get started here, I have to know something. How'd you recognize me back in the lobby?"

"How do you think I recognized you?" the man said. "I saw your picture in the paper yesterday, and I've been waiting for you to show up here ever since. You know that picture you took

THE LAST FRAME 93

Thursday night—the shot of the kid trying to jump off the George Washington Bridge? That's why I'm upset.''

"Hey, I was upset, too. It only ran in two editions."

The man started biting his right index finger, trying to stay in control. "Stow it, smartass. That kid is my son. And I want to know what right you had to take his picture."

Ah, Carver thought, the old sore-relative bit. Carver had run into his kind before, and you couldn't smooth-talk them. You had to set them straight.

"Let me tell you a little story, sir, and all I ask is that you hear me out. Know the joke about the black guy and the motel pool down South?"

The man responded by standing up to leave, but Carver gestured him to stay. "Hold your hat. I said to hear me out. I'm not trying to draw a laugh. I'm telling you this to make a point.

"There's this roadside motel in Georgia with a swimming pool in the courtyard. One morning the manager knocks on this black guest's door and asks him to leave. The black guy demands to know why: 'It's because I'm black, isn't it?'

"The manager says no, that's not it at all. It's just not the kind of thing he likes to talk about—just pack your bags and leave. The black guy keeps pressing him, so the manager finally blurts: 'I saw you pissing in the pool.'

"The black guy is flabbergasted. 'Come on, man. Everybody pisses in the pool.'

" 'Yeah,' the manager says, 'but not from the high dive.' "

The man seated across the table from Carver was not amused. He sat there, shredding a napkin for a moment or two, then asked: "And just what does this have to do with my son?"

"If your son wants to kill himself, fine," Carver replied. "That's his business. But not when he does it from the high dive. If he wants to kill himself on the George Washington Bridge at rush hour, back up traffic for four miles, and have two policemen risk their lives trying to stop him, then it's everybody's business."

The man stood again.

Carver kept talking: "You can leave if you want to, but I'm not done. Here's my point. If your son really wanted to commit suicide, he would've blown out his brains in your basement. When he went to the bridge, he was asking for help. He's sick.''

"He's sick? You're the one making a buck off it."

"You're absolutely right," Carver said as he stood to leave. "Have a nice day."

Chapter Twenty-three

Lest his conscience get the better of him, Will Carver tried to dismiss the conversation with the jumper's father by blaming it on somebody else—the *Daily News*. Soon as he got off the elevator on the seventh floor, he bumped into Ralph Dempsey and got ready to read him the riot act for not having better security by the front entrance.

Ralph was in one of his pissant moods. "Well, if it isn't F. Stop Fitzgerald?"

Carver ignored the sarcasm. "Before you start in, Ralph, I want to know why the hell you ran my picture and that story with my byline yesterday. Now I'll have half the creeps in the world comin' after me for some long-forgotten picture I took."

"Cool off," Ralph said. "I can't help it that when you make news you make the *News*. If you want to get into gunfights, that's your problem."

Poor timing. Ralph, too, was clearly having a bad day. Ralph was never what you'd call a sharp dresser, but today he resembled a Canal Street fire sale. His electric-blue shirt was pitted out, his tie was askew, and his pants had horizontal creases across the thighs from sitting at a VDT too long.

Since today was Sunday, the source of his exasperation probably wasn't another purge in Editorial, or word of some other budget slashing. After several years of red ink, the *Daily News* had begun to thrive again, and management wanted to keep it that way. Chances were likelier Ralph was tired from working the weekend. Maybe it was just a slow news day, which meant no big murders or terrorist attacks to run on Page One. Ralph would have to run some dull federal-deficit story big, and newsstand sales would slacken tomorrow. The New York *Post* never had that problem. On slow news days, the *Post* would just invent a big story or two.

"So, Carver, tell me about last night."

"Aren't you supposed to be off tonight?"

"I was, but Dwayne called in sick, and I had a chance to rack up some overtime. But let's not change the subject. What about last night?"

"Meaning what?"

"Meaning the guy you left for dead on the Lower East Side."

"I'll tell you about it in due time—especially if you had a reporter come up with that phone number for me."

"I guess we got a deal, then," Ralph said. "The reporter did get a phone number for you, and he'd like to talk to you later about a second-day story."

"Who's the reporter?"

"Doug Scarpetti."

"Better make it a third-day story. That guy's slower than a crosstown bus."

"Meanwhile, Carver, before I forget, your alleged FBI agent who was in yesterday looking for you—he seemed extremely displeased that you never showed up, and he took it out on me. You owe me."

"What did he want?"

"He asked about your background, any mob ties, and why you were there when the guy in the Cherokee crashed. I said you ran the guy off the road."

"Yeah, you got that right," Carver said. "By the way, the other reason I'm here: You got any money for me?"

Ralph shuffled some papers. A bad sign.

"It's Sunday, Carver. Maybe tomorrow, but you'll be lucky if you get it then. The latest word from the publisher's office is to stretch all payments to free-lancers. I'm bucking it like crazy, but the bottom-line boys are running the show these days. They want to keep showing a profit."

"Terrific."

"Hey, don't get snotty. You're pulling down some major dinero here. Last time I checked, we owed you over a grand. That's serious dough for a few photos. Heck, in the old days, the *News* paid diddly—a dollar for a one-alarm fire, two bucks for two alarms, et cetera. And those gangland slayings you love—some places paid by the bullet hole. Unless your subject was machine-gunned, you were talking petty cash."

"Ralph, that was the thirties. The nation was still on the gold standard. This is now, and I'm broke. Can you at least lend me fifty dollars to tide me over? Then I'll get out of your hair."

Ralph pulled out his wallet and removed three twenties. "Here. Now do me a favor and shoot somebody quick—and I'm not talking about using a camera. If something doesn't break soon, we'll have to lead with the Jets' latest disaster tomorrow, and I'll spend my day off fielding phone calls from the managing editor, who blames me personally when genuine tragedy doesn't strike."

"Can't help you right now," Carver replied. "But I might have something later in the week."

Chapter Twenty-four

When he walked into the morgue, Will Carver took one look around him and got depressed. It hadn't changed much over the years, but he sensed the old days ending. Reporters called the place a library now, and it looked and felt like one—wood had given way to walnut-grained Formica, and some of the files were on microfiche, and air-conditioning had replaced opening a window.

It would soon get worse. Scuttlebutt had it that the library was on the verge of total extinction, little more than a repository for the relics of the glory days of the *News*. Soon reporters wouldn't come in here to check out clips anymore. They'd call them up electronically on their VDTs.

Times had changed the *News* and its entire operation. "New York's Picture Newspaper," the *News* called itself, but if people wanted pictures they watched TV. As a result, the paper had been struggling since the late sixties, and only shrewd new management had gotten it back on its feet. Nowadays, news executives and ad directors discussed upgrading the product as though they were printing a better brand of place mat.

At one point, it had gotten so bad that the real estate the paper owned was worth more than the paper itself. The printing presses on the second and third floors had been jettisoned—to make room for office space. The paper was beamed electronically to three remote printing plants, and the old hum in the newsroom had vanished.

Veteran reporters joked that newspapers had become dinosaurs, and the only reasons people bought a paper anymore were the daily lottery numbers, TV listings, sports, and food coupons. Carver suspected the reporters were right—to a degree. Those were the reasons people had always bought newspapers.

The library was deserted, so Carver walked around the Formica-topped checkout desk to the shelves behind. He removed the reverse directory for Manhattan (it sat on the third shelf, just above *The Handbook of Literary Curiosities*) and went to work, but his heart wasn't in it.

His conscience was bugging him again, and that depressed him. Journalists can't have consciences, at least not if they want to stay in hard news. He thought of the jumper's father again, and remembered the last time he'd used a reverse directory. It had been four years ago. He'd almost gotten a rape victim killed.

Carver had lived in the detective bureau of the Sixth Precinct station house then, and he awoke one morning to news of an assault in progress on West Fourteenth.

Some crackpot had abducted a deli counter girl on her coffee break and taken her at gunpoint to his flat on the fringe of the Tenderloin District. Neighbors heard the screams and, in a rare display of civic duty, actually called the police.

By the time Carver got there—he drove a thirdhand Pinto in those days—the cops had a siege on their hands. The lunatic insisted that if the cops tried to storm him, he'd shoot the girl.

Carver returned to the Pinto and checked the apartment number in his reverse directory. He mounted his two-hundred-millimeter lens on his Canon and went to the pay phone across the street from siege central. The guy answered the phone on the second ring.

"Hey, turkey, this is the police," Carver said. It wasn't the first time he'd lied in the line of duty. "We got your ass surrounded. You don't have a dog's chance in China of coming out alive—unless you come to the front window and talk out a deal for the girl."

Carver figured that when the guy came to the window to negotiate, he'd get a dramatic shot for the next day's paper. The trouble was, the guy wasn't in a bargaining mood. Instead, the guy opened fire on the girl.

The cops went into their Israeli commando act—deep down,

they'd been dying to anyway. They smashed the door from its hinges and blasted the crazed bastard out of his pointy-toed shoes. He was dead before his body hit the wall.

Carver raced across the street. By the time he reached the landing, the cops were carrying out the girl.

She wasn't nearly as upset about the hole in her stomach as she was about the police: "You morons. He was going to give up till you made that phone call."

The cops didn't know what she was talking about.

Carver went upstairs and got to work. Because of the telephoto lens, Carver had to shoot the guy from the hallway, and he had always felt that the photo that ran in the *News* suffered for it.

Worse, one of the cops saw the reverse directory on the front seat of Carver's car and figured out Carver must have been the one who'd made the call to the kidnapper, which explained why Carver now lived in the Ninth Precinct station house instead of the Sixth, and how he'd come to meet Gina. . . .

Now, as he thumbed through the directory, he hoped that he wouldn't get any innocent people shot this time around. First he checked the phone number Mo Orsinski had called the night before. The number belonged to Brud Siracusa, address in some Village high rise. He checked the clip files for a Brud Siracusa, but came up empty.

Next he looked up the Jane Street address in the reverse directory and found three apartments, three names, three phone numbers. He wrote them on the back of an envelope he retrieved from a wastepaper basket: Frank Humphreys, Eric Lynnsey, and the Other Self Ltd.

An excellent chance existed that either the blackmail photos had been taken in one of the three apartments or that the blackmailer had visited or lived in one of those apartments. Those photos . . . Something in the back of his mind kept connecting them with the photos he was assembling for his book. He had to get both sets of photos together as soon as he could. That's when he called the police.

Chapter Twenty-five

When he stopped at the wire-photo machine in the newsroom, Will Carver felt a tap on his shoulder.

It was Randall, a copyboy and occasional drinking buddy. Carver took one more look at a photo of the latest breakout of hostilities between Iran and Iraq, then threw it into the trash. Nobody ran 'em anyway. They just weren't news anymore.

"What's up, R-Man? I probably can't help you out. I'm short on cash myself."

Randall frowned. "Carver, I probably have more money on me than you do. I wanted to know if Ralph told you about the fed who came asking about you yesterday. Well, the guy told me to call him as soon as you showed up, or I'd catch major heat. What do I do?"

"Let me see the phone number." It was the same one Mo Orsinski had dialed the night before: Carver was finally getting somewhere.

"You know the threat's pure hooey," Carver said. "But sooner or later I'm going to have to talk to this geek. Could you do me a favor? Call the guy and tell him I'll meet him tomorrow, ten A.M., in the art biography section at the Strand Book store. I'll be the only guy wearing a Phillies cap."

Lieutenant Joe Gold had been about to go to dinner when Carver called. Gold decided to forgo the pastrami to find out what his old buddy was up to, but he felt awkward. Carver no doubt assumed Joe was doing him a favor, but Gold had sensed something wrong and wanted to find out more.

101

First, there had to be more to the shooting at the pawnshop than Carver had let on. Then there'd been that guy nearly strangled in the Nova last night. Gold had arrived at the scene just after the reporter called, and there was a big hubbub over the "I killed Bingo" scratched on the door. Everybody figured it had to be a mob job, and Joe didn't say anything to disabuse them of their theory.

Truth was, the mob would have used a .22 and executed the guy. As for the "I killed Bingo" on the car door, it made Gold think. He couldn't help but recall when he'd still walked patrol over in the Sixth Precinct and he and Carver would go for a few beers after his shift ended.

That had been eight years ago, when Carver was reveling in his bum-photographer routine and all he could talk about was the exploits of an old photographer named Weegee. His favorite story was how Weegee was tapped into Murder, Inc., and how they'd tell him when and where they were dumping a body.

According to Carver, the boys would steal a car, scratch "Ice Wagon" on the side, and park it by a cemetery or funeral parlor. Weegee, however, wasn't satisfied knowing where the body would be—he got word to the mob that they should steal gray cars instead of black ones because gray showed up better in his pictures.

Because of that story, Gold sensed that Carver had been involved in last night's antics. It didn't add up. Carver never struck Joe Gold as a hoodlum, but then Gold didn't know Carver like he once did. And he didn't want to. Truth was, Carver had become an embarrassment. If Downtown got wind of Carver sleeping under a desk in the narcotics room, Gold would be the one to give him the boot. He'd been meaning to anyway, but old friendships were tough to end.

Joe Gold had been parked outside the *News* for five minutes when he saw Carver push through the revolving door. Joe tooted the horn, and Carver ran over, all smiles.

"Hey, bub, thanks for doing this," Carver said, and slid onto the front seat next to Joe.

"What's the scoop?"

"I need to pick up some stuff at my apartment, and I'm afraid somebody might be waiting for me. I'm on MacDougal Street, just north of Bleecker.''

Joe shifted the car into drive and turned onto Third Avenue. He tried to stay as low-keyed as he could. ''Sounds serious. Care to fill me in?''

Carver put him off. ''No, it's personal. I'll tell you after it blows over.''

''Hey, you read about the guy left for dead on East Third last night?'' Joe offered.

''I read about it in today's paper. Wished I'd been there. Hell of a photo.''

At the next red light, Joe Gold started to draw out Carver more. ''Yeah, I was there. The weird thing was, I thought of you immediately.''

Gold glanced at his passenger, but Carver was looking out the window, the brim of his Phillies cap pressed against the glass.

''What do you mean?'' Carver finally responded.

''I remember when we'd go drinking and you'd talk about Weegee and the old 'Ice Wagon' bit. That car on East Third had a message scratched on the side, too.''

''No fooling. Didn't see it in the paper.''

''Then you weren't involved, right?''

''Right.''

When the blue-and-white reached Fourteenth Street, Joe turned and headed west. ''So tell me again. What's up at your place?''

''I need some photographs. Remember I told you my place was ransacked on Thursday? I have some valuable pictures stashed away there, and I better get 'em before these guys come back. While we're talking favors, I've got to ask you for another big one. Remember how my car disappeared Friday amid all the commotion at Bingo's Pawnshop? Turns out the car wasn't stolen. One of your buddies towed it.''

''Must have been a new guy. My guys know not to tow your car.''

''Can you get it back for me?''

''Sorry, but getting your car towed is like getting a vasectomy—once it's done, it's usually irreversible.''

''Right—and in both cases there's always a prick involved.''

Gold bit his lip. "Carver, I'm doing you a favor, so don't give me any crap, all right?"

"Does that mean you'll get my car?"

"No. It means you'll be on foot for a while. Nobody can get a car out of the pound without paying. Nobody."

"No harm in asking."

The two men fell silent until they reached MacDougal Street. Joe Gold reached under the dash, flicked on the flashing lights, and explained: "If anyone's waiting, this'll scare them off."

Gold double-parked the blue-and-white in front of Carver's apartment building. The afternoon's warmth had disappeared with the sun, and Gold turned up the collar on his jacket as he left the squad car.

The apartment was on the second floor, and it sounded like somebody was home. Gold could hear the country music from out in the hall.

"Company?"

"No, security."

Gold looked baffled, and entering the apartment didn't help. Inside the door was a trash can brimming with beer bottles and empty cottage cheese containers. A pile of TV dinner trays sat in the sink, as though Carver planned to reuse them.

Joe stood by the door while Carver went into the next room. When Gold heard talking, he looked inside and said to Carver, "So you do have company."

"No, just talking to my pal. Hermit crab named Port Authority. That's the only place you can get crabs bigger than him," Carver said, waiting for a laugh. It never arrived.

Gold tugged on his ear impatiently. "Let's get your photos and get out. I have to get back to the station house." Gold looked around. An old orange crate for a coffee table. Beat-up couch. A few newspapers on the linoleum floor. "You always leave the radio on while you're away?"

"Yeah, country music station. I figure people'll think I'm home, and armed."

Joe Gold forced a smile: Carver was stranger than he'd thought.

Carver walked past him to the kitchen and went over to the

toilet, which stood by the stove and a clunky old camera on a tripod.

Gold was going to say something, but Carver cut him short. "Don't say it. I know, never crap where you eat. I didn't design this place. I only rent it." Carver lifted the tank lid and placed it upside down on the stove. Taped to it was a clear plastic bag with photos inside.

"Always keep your work in the toilet?"

"Isn't that where you say my stuff belongs?"

Gold smiled genuinely, and Carver removed the photos from the bag. He offered Gold a look. Gold sat at the kitchen table and leafed through them while Carver went to feed his pet crab. The photos weren't Hallmark card material, but Joe sat transfixed by the images: a corpse lying in a pool of blood outside a flophouse, a battered suspect behind bars at the station house, kids playing jump rope in a glass-strewn alley. New York, New York.

Chapter Twenty-six

Brud Siracusa called Mo as soon as he'd hung up on the copyboy at the *News*. The kid hadn't called when Carver showed up in the newsroom as promised, but the kid had done just as good—he had passed along a message from Carver that he'd be at the Strand at ten A.M. to hand over the pictures, and then they'd be all set.

For toppers, after the kid obviously had told Carver that Brud was looking for him, the kid had the nerve to ask when he'd get the other twenty bucks that Brud had offered as part of the deal. Brud had come up with the perfect answer: "I'll give your money to Carver tomorrow morning, and he can drop it off." Right, and the check is in the mail, and the Yankees will be in the World Series next year with George Steinbrenner at the helm.

Cripes, it was eight P.M., and he had a full night's worth of calls to make—to Mo, to Tracey, and to the mark. Better keep the conversations short. It would be a long Monday.

"Hey, Mo. I got a message from Carver, and we're back in business. Meet me at the office tomorrow morning, nine o'clock, and work out the last details then. How'd the collections go this afternoon? . . . Fifteen hundred bucks? Hell, I might even tell my uncle about half of it—and we can still pocket seven hundred and fifty of the take. You know what they say. When you're hot, you're Brud. . . . Yeah, catch you tomorrow."

The call to Tracey went as easily. They agreed that they'd still give the mark till Tuesday evening to drop off the money, so he'd have plenty of time to come up with the full amount.

Then Brud made the big call, not dreading it nearly as much

as he had expected. "Hello, Mrs. Stanten. Sorry to be calling Mr. Stanten about work on a Sunday evening, but I wanted to get things squared away for a big meeting we have scheduled for tomorrow morning. He'll know what it's about. . . . Yeah, I can wait a minute."

Damned rich people, having supper at eight-thirty on a Sunday night. Probably came from a chamber music concert, or some other yawn pastime.

Stanten finally came on the line, sounding irritated about having his dinner disturbed, but Brud jumped right in. "Mr. Stanten, you may not remember me, but you will. I met you at that bar last Tuesday. . . . No, I can't call you tomorrow at the office. I can talk to you now. Don't hang up. You'll want to hear all of this. I'm calling you with some good news. Remember when you went back to that apartment with your playmate? I took some pictures, and they came out just fabulous. I'd give you a set of prints for nothin', but they cost so much to develop, I thought I'd just sell you the whole lot—pix and negatives. How's two hundred and fifty sound? Two hundred and fifty grand, of course."

The rich boy was starting to whine, said he couldn't possibly find that kind of money. Brud said nothing, just let the guy twist in the wind. After what seemed twenty seconds of silence, Stanten wanted to know when he had to come up with the money.

"Tuesday evening. At your favorite pick-up bar. By seven. Small bills, unmarked—but you've seen enough movies to know how it's done. If you leave the cops out of this, I'll leave your board of directors out of this, even though the pix would look simply grand in your personnel folder, wouldn't they? Leave the money with the bartender, and he'll give you a sealed manila envelope with everything you'll need. Questions? . . . I didn't think so. You take care now, you hear?"

After he'd hung up the phone, Brud thought back to the evening at the bar when Tracey had pointed out Stanten. The guy was wearing a fancy getup, ready for a big night on the town, but he was avoiding the regulars. He stood by himself in the corner, pumping quarter after quarter into the bar's only pinball machine.

Brud knew a chump when he saw one. He walked over to watch.

Stanten ignored him and kept playing. He stood awkwardly at the machine, one foot behind the other, lurching forward as he worked the flipper buttons. He'd get off a shot or two before the shiny steel ball disappeared off the bottom of the playfield.

The game was a classic Williams machine called "High Ace," and Brud had played it enough to know that this guy didn't stand a chance the way he played. After the fifth ball promptly skidded down a side gutter, Brud introduced himself as Terry. The man said that his name was Sal, but Brud knew he was lying, too. Nobody at Tracey's place ever used his real name.

"Well, Sal, can I offer you a suggestion or two? You're too uptight. You're not shaking hands with a maiden aunt here. You've got to play rough if you want to get anywhere."

The man blushed. "But if you play rough, won't the machine tilt or something?" The man's high-pitched voice grated on Brud's ears.

"Not if you know how to play the game. The machine doesn't want to be treated nice. You have to knock it around a little, put your body into it, if you want it to put out. You play entirely by the rules, you never make the big score. You got to know when to go easy and when to bang away. Pinball's like life, Sal. If you let me, I'll teach you a little something about both."

Stanten smiled sheepishly. Brud knew the real game was about to begin.

Chapter Twenty-seven

The conversation lasted all of ten minutes, but Gina Constantine feared her tone of voice was giving her away. Why were men so impossible to talk to? She didn't know quite what to say tonight, so she tried to make him do most of the talking. Yet near the end, when he said he loved her, she found herself saying she loved him, too.

Then click and relief. Postponing the inevitable was so much easier by long-distance—no direct eye contact with Steve, no facial expressions that showed how she felt anymore.

Besides, Gina told herself, deep down everybody knew that saying "I love you" by phone was like saying "I love you" in the sack: Nobody could ever hold you to it.

She reached into the refrigerator for the two-liter bottle of Tab and poured herself a glass. She looked at her watch. Midnight, and Carver was nowhere to be found. So much for a nice restaurant dinner.

Sundays were always the worst, but on this night Gina felt more depressed than usual. Steve's phone call was part of it, she understood that much, but she sensed that her relationship with him only reflected her situation in general. She tried to think of the navy term her father used to use to describe it. Dry dock. She was in emotional dry dock, and with no real opportunity or desire to have it any other way.

Gina had been seeing Steve long-distance for almost a year. They'd met on a plane to the Bahamas last January. She'd gone at her mother's insistence: "Isn't it time you got on with your life?" her mother kept asking, and then suggested the Bahamas as a place to meet someone new. After the vacation, she and Steve had kept in touch by phone and started sharing a weekend at his place every couple of months. He lived outside Baltimore, almost four hours by train. He had a solid job designing assault vehicles for a Defense Department contractor, he had a brick tudor in one of the nicer subdivisions to the northwest, and he had a five-year-old son by the inevitable first marriage.

He was a solid citizen—always used a turn signal, even when the road was empty. Sensible, fair, undemanding. She offered him companionship every few weekends, someone to phone to discuss life's potholes. He offered her assurance that she was still attractive, a justification for not dating more often, and an excuse when a patrolman would ask her out. It was so easy: "Sorry, but I'm already seeing someone."

She and Steve hadn't really talked about marriage, but Steve didn't seem to consider it out of the question, especially if she were willing to move to Baltimore. And that was the rub. He thought she was crazy to live in New York, and she thought it would be crazy to live anywhere else.

But there was more to it. More and more, she was finding herself in the same situation she used to face at her old high school dances. . . . It'd be a slow dance, and most of the other students would pair off, and she knew if she didn't find a partner soon she'd be sitting out the rest of the evening.

Even so, she was starting to admit to herself that she didn't care enough for Steve. The realization came to her just minutes before, when the phone rang. She had hoped it was Will Carver and it turned out to be Steve.

She even had to concede that she liked being with Will Carver, at least in small doses, but common sense kept telling her not to get involved. It wasn't because he had a streak of bizarre behavior (although he did). It was because at the rate he was going he'd be dead soon.

She looked at her watch again. He was late—and she wondered if he was dead already. She remembered that this was how she always felt when her husband was on duty. She remembered that one night she had been right.

With that, the phone rang. This time it was Carver. She smiled to herself until he said he had bumped into a friend, they'd decided to drink a few beers, and he wouldn't be back till later. And, by the way, would she mind calling the station house and running checks on the guy in the Cherokee and a guy named Brud Siracusa, and, tomorrow morning, would she retrieve the camera and the blackmail photographs at the station house? He told her where he hid his desk key, then said good-bye.

Gina hung up, reached for her Tab, and wondered whether a nice house in Baltimore might not be so bad after all.

Chapter Twenty-eight

Monday Morning

The Strand Bookstore at Twelfth and Broadway has one of the largest assortments of used books in the world, more than a million volumes on four floors. On any given day it has every English-language book ever printed, except for the ones you're looking for.

So you browse, scanning stack after stack, and when it's time to leave two hours later, you purchase thirty dollars' worth of books you'll never read but can't pass up. It's as much a Manhattan tradition as transit strikes and alternate-side-of-the-street parking tickets.

Will Carver liked to spend rainy afternoons at the Strand. He'd thumb through old photography books for ideas. The more he looked, the more certain he was that all the great photographs already had been taken—that most new photographs were merely the old ones taken from new angles, or with new subjects. He'd look at a monograph by Diane Arbus and think of Arbus's mentor, Lisette Model. Then he'd look at pictures by Model and think of Weegee. Then he'd think of Weegee and . . .

He had killed so many hours at the Strand that he found it strange to go there on business. Yet as he walked up Broadway, he was calmer than he'd expected. At this point he was ready to surrender the photos just to have this guy Brud off his back. Life's too short to deal with complete jerks, Carver figured. Life's too short, period. The expression made him recall an old John Hiatt tune called "Slow Turning," and he hummed it in his mind's ear as he walked the final blocks up Broadway.

> Time is short and here's the damn thing about it
> You're gonna die, gonna die for sure
> And you can learn to live with love or without it
> But there ain't no cure.

Carver decided he'd learned to live without it, especially after the reception Gina Constantine had given him when he knocked on her door at two-thirty A.M. Women were universally strange, Carver concluded. One minute they wanted nothing to do with you, and the next they wanted to know why you were late.

Gina made him sleep on the couch last night, which hadn't helped his back any. Then, when he awoke as she was about to go out this morning and he reminded her about running that errand at the station house, she merely slammed the door.

Carver couldn't worry about it now. At ten A.M. sharp, he entered the Strand. He walked past the metal detector and the half-price review coupons by the door, past the cashiers, and saw Mo Orsinski ahead of him, feigning interest in a book in the photography section. The place smelled like a carton of books in a musty basement. Actually, it was a few steps removed.

Mo looked up and said with a smile: "Good morning, dipstick. I got someone I want you to meet." And he clasped his right hand on Carver's bicep.

Carver looked to his left. A few yards away stood a blond-haired man that Carver guessed to be in his mid- to late twenties. An expensive camel hair overcoat was draped over the man's shoulders, and contempt hung from the corners of his mouth. The man stood with Italian loafers planted two feet apart, gunslinger style. The man's hands were planted on the waist of his pleated brown flannel slacks.

Carver had frequented enough after-hours bars to peg the guy immediately—a hotheaded bully who courted trouble just for the chance to flex his muscles. Carver also knew the only way to handle jerks of his ilk was to ignore them completely or stand your ground and take any lumps that came your way. He decided upon the latter.

No one spoke.

Carver looked back to Mo, who sported his very best glare and squeezed Carver's bicep harder until Brud broke the silence. "Party's over, dipstick. Hand over the pictures."

Carver tugged his arm free and looked at Brud. "Tell our friend to back off."

Brud nodded to Mo, who retreated two paces and leaned on a table brimming with remaindered hardbacks.

Carver forced a smile. "I've looked forward to meeting you— you are the famous Brud Siracusa, are you not? Don't be startled. You've been leaving your greasy palm prints all over town."

Brud bit his lower lip and regained the same steely gaze that a dentist has when he's got a drill in his hand and his wife's interior decorator in the chair. "Stow the smartass remarks. We have business to discuss. Now please come quietly."

"Sorry, Brud, but I'd just as soon talk right here." Carver pointed to a room marked ART BIOGRAPHY. "How about in there? Nobody'll be able to hear us."

Once inside the closet-size room, Carver leaned against one of the floor-to-ceiling stacks. "Now what can I do for you?"

"We'll make this simple, dipstick," Brud said. "You bought a hot camera at Bingo's Pawnshop. The roll of film inside belongs to me. I want it back. Now."

"I'd love to help, but I don't have the film."

"Get it."

"I can't right now."

"Bull crap."

"Think whatever you like. The negatives are locked in a safe-deposit box, and I keep the key at the *Daily News*."

Brud pulled out a thin gold case and extracted a brown cigarette. "You better not be jerking my chain, and I'll tell you why. I'm allergic to dogs, Mr. Carver. Always have been. Usually it's not a problem. I just avoid 'em. But every so often, I have to deal with them, and it makes me sick."

Carver looked at his watch. "What's the point?"

"Let me go on. I used to work construction, Mr. Carver. Back-breaking work. The pay was lousy. I had to bring my own lunch in a paper bag."

Mo lit Brud's cigarette, and Brud took a deep drag before continuing. "One day I decided to live it up, stopped at a deli on my way to the work site. Bought this overstuffed corned beef sandwich. So I get to work and put my paper sack next to the other guys' lunch boxes. I get my hammer and start nailing huge sheets of plywood to the frame, hour after hour, till my arms are killing me. I'm working up an appetite, can't wait to taste that sandwich. Then I happen to look up as this floppy-eared mutt grabs my lunch bag and takes off. I race after him until I finally have him cornered."

Brud paused to take a drag from the cigarette. "Dog thinks I'm playing, right? Lunch bag in his mouth, frisky wag in his tail. I wave my hammer at him and tell him to drop my lunch, but he just keeps wagging that tail. Trouble is, I'm allergic to dogs. They make me sick. I ask for my lunch again; he refuses. So I have no choice. I give him the hammer—right to the head—and I take my lunch.

"I guess the point here, Mr. Carver, is you're beginning to make me sick. I have a hammer. You have my lunch. What'll it be?"

Carver wished he were anywhere else, and nervously tugged on his shirt collar. "I said I'd get the pictures for you. What else can I tell you?"

Brud flicked an ash onto the floor. "Just so you understand. I'm a reasonable man; I'll make you a reasonable offer. You want to buy some time, no problem. Just make sure you get the film and a set of prints and leave the whole works wrapped in a newspaper in the entrance to the church on Stuyvesant Square—East Sixteenth Street just off Second Avenue—in two hours."

Carver shook his head. "No can do. Give me till five. But what if I've grown attached to them?"

"Keep a set for yourself, if you like. I don't give a crap. They mean nothing to you. If you're an intelligent man, you will surrender them. If you're an ignorant man . . . I know where you live. I know where you work. And next time I use the hammer."

Carver rubbed his chin appreciatively, stalling for time. Clearly this conversation wasn't going to end in a handshake.

"Maybe this will help you make up your mind." Brud nodded toward the doorway. Carver turned in time to see Mo's fist arrive. The impact sent Carver crashing sideways into the stacks.

"That's for the rat trap," Mo said.

Carver's knees wobbled. Mo pounded Carver's face again. "And that's for nearly choking me to death."

Carver staggered. A browser took one step into the tiny room, recognized trouble, and beat a hasty exit.

When the coast was clear again, Brud said, "Pay attention. I'm through fiddling around with you. I want that film and I'll go to any length to get it back. Any length." He spat the last two words for emphasis.

Carver wiped his nose and saw blood on his hand. His knees buckled again, and Brud grabbed a fistful of Carver's peacoat to keep him from caving to the floor.

"Five o'clock. Stuyvesant Square." Brud pushed Carver against the stacks, then dropped his cigarette and crushed it. "See you real soon."

Chapter Twenty-nine

Will Carver was applying a towel filled with ice to his nose when Gina arrived. She was clutching the camera and photos from his desk in the narcotics room at the station house, and she almost seemed glad to see him until he lowered the towel and she saw the swollen cheekbone and the blood caked on his upper lip.

"Will, what happened to you?"

Carver tried to act natural, but his eyes welled up and he looked away. "Sometimes you get the elevator, sometimes you get the shaft."

"What are you talking about?"

He put the cold compress back on his nose. She lay her hand gently on his shoulder, but he shrugged it aside.

"Will, talk to me."

"Give me a minute. I'll be all right."

He sat on the sofa and caught his breath. "I met our blackmailer this morning. Young hothead named Brud Siracusa. You know—the guy I asked you to check up on."

Carver put the compress back on his nose for a moment, then continued. "You know, I actually was toying with the idea of giving him the freaking photos and be done with it, but then Siracusa's batboy worked me over. What do they say about mad dogs—either kill them or leave them alone? I should have killed Mo Saturday night when I had a chance."

He asked if she had any aspirin, and she returned with a dime store tumbler filled with water and four tablets. He downed all four with one gulp. "Don't worry. I'll live. As I was about to ask, you find anything on Siracusa?"

"Not much. Had an assault charge filed against him two years ago, but it never went to trial. Apparently he manages a few apartment buildings in the Village, and he pulled a knife on a tenant. The guy dropped the charges—Siracusa probably bought him off with a few months' free rent. Meanwhile, you were right about the Nova. Hot. Read an item in the *News* this morning. But nobody can prove your pal Mo stole the car. He's off the hook."

"I know. The reporter got most of that stuff from me. What else you got?"

"Still no word on the stiff in the Cherokee. Police in Harlem are checking, which means forget it. The computers have been down, the guy may not have been fingerprinted, and nobody's come in to claim him. Don't hold your breath. In Harlem, dead bodies are the least of their worries. Here are your photos. You're right—they're disgusting. But I couldn't find the negatives you wanted. I searched both drawers."

The clock on the end table started to chime, and Carver waited for it to finish before answering. "Nuts. What a dunce I am. I never store my photos and negatives together—in case of fire or theft. Or photographer's paranoia. And I just remembered where I hid them. Tucked under the passenger seat in my Rabbit."

"So get your car out of the pound today."

"I'm broke. The *News* didn't have my money last night."

"Then let me float you that loan I offered you."

"I never borrow money."

"Don't be asinine."

Carver rubbed the stubble on his chin and sighed. "Let's forget it for now, okay? Let me get some coffee, and we'll look over those photos. Maybe we're missing something."

In the kitchen, he found a jar of instant coffee, filled the tumbler with hot water, and dumped in some crystals.

Gina stood next to the couch and scanned the photos spread on the coffee table.

"I don't get it," Gina said upon his return. "These pictures—you can't see the guy's face, only the woman's. How could the guy be blackmailed, unless he didn't know his face wasn't visible? I don't get it."

Carver leaned over and looked at the pictures. "Sorry, you got me on this one. Maybe the woman's being blackmailed—or her husband is."

"We have to keep looking," she insisted. "The answer has to be staring us in the face. The camera never lies."

"I hate to disillusion you, but the camera is the biggest liar ever invented," he replied, and sat beside her. "It doesn't capture reality. It records the amounts of light bouncing off an image. No light, no picture.

"And while the camera's shutter clicks open for a split second so the light can expose the film inside, that light is getting bent all out of shape by all the concave and convex pieces of glass in the lens. To top it off, the impression the light leaves behind is upside down and backwards. That's why it's called a negative—black is white and white is black."

Gina started to speak, but he cut her off: "When you transfer the image from the negative to a sheet of photographic paper, you can cheat further by cropping out parts of the picture. All you can see is what the photographer wants you to.

"Or you see something else entirely. When you see a picture of vanilla ice cream in a magazine, you're probably looking at mashed potatoes. Real ice cream melts too fast under the studio's lights. It's like what the photographer Diane Arbus once said: A photograph is a secret about a secret. The more it tells you, the less you know."

Gina studied the photos again, but it didn't help. "So what are you saying? The naked eye is blind? The man isn't a man? The woman isn't a woman?"

That was all Carver needed.

He held one of the photos five inches from his eyes and stared for a moment. "You got it. Sometimes I'm as dumb as I look. What we have here isn't vanilla ice cream. It's mashed potatoes."

Gina took the shot and stared at it. "Will, am I missing something?"

"Like the old saying goes, that woman is no lady. Take a look. The Adam's apple, the arms, everything. It's a transvestite. I told you I thought she looked vaguely familiar. I took a shot of this drag queen for a book I'm working on. Drunk in a transvestite bar in the West Village. Didn't even know I was taking his picture. Place called Acey-Deucey's. That's what the jerk in the Jeep was talking about before he died. Queens. Acey's."

Carver took a final sip of coffee, then stood. "And as for the apartments on Jane Street where Puma stole the camera with the blackmail photos"—he reached into his peacoat for his reporter's notepad—"I bet you dollars to doilies that one of them belongs to some transvestite group. . . . Here. The Other Self Ltd."

He walked to the phone and dialed the number. A gentle voice answered on the third ring.

"Hello. My name is Carver. Will Carver. Perhaps you've heard the name? I write for the *Voice*, and we're doing our annual story on services for gays and transvestites. Someone said I should give you a call. . . . Well, when will someone who *can* answer my questions be available? . . . But you do provide services for transvestites, right? Thank you. I'll call back tomorrow."

He hung up and beamed—until Gina said, "You have to go to the police."

"Spoken like a true policewoman," Carver said. "But I can't. What do I have here? A bunch of dirty pictures. That's sick maybe, but it's not illegal. The guy in the picture may have been set up, but he hasn't been blackmailed that I know of. And I couldn't begin to connect any of this with Bingo's death.

"Besides, you seem to forget I nearly choked some guy to death on account of these photos. The cops'll find out all of that if I go to them."

Gina held her ground. "You've got to show these photos to Joe Gold. Turn this over to the pros."

"What will Joe do with the photos—besides pass 'em around the station house for grins? If the police do find the transvestite in the photos, the guy's secret will be all over town and he'll be ruined. He may be a hurting cowpoke, but nobody deserves to be destroyed like that."

Gina went into her staring-out-the-window routine, a sure sign that he was losing this argument.

Carver pleaded with her. "Look at me. You're absolutely right. I should have gone to the cops long ago and been done with it. But now it's too late. I have to deal with it on my own. I've got to stall Brud."

Gina seemed confused. "What good will that do?"

"If I do have to give up the blackmail photos, at least maybe I can buy enough time to find this transvestite and warn him. He might be able to cover his tracks, get out of town. . . ."

"And if you fail?"

"At least by dealing with Brud, the guy has a chance to decide what it's worth to keep his little fetish a secret—"

"Or a chance to hang himself," Gina interrupted. "When you get right down to it, the identity of this guy is immaterial. If you burn the pictures, it doesn't matter who he is. He can't get blackmailed."

"Siracusa thinks I'm going to give him the pictures. He may have made contact with the poor fool already, for all we know. That would explain why Siracusa's being such a hardass. He must have a deadline. Face it. If I destroy the pictures, there's nothing stopping Siracusa from trying again. Or finding some other chump."

Gina looked out the window again. The wind was whipping out of the west, and she watched as two businessmen clutched the brims of their hats to keep them from blowing away in a gust.

Carver kept talking. "In the meantime, the pictures are my only bargaining chip. It won't be the end of the world if I do have to part with them. Like Brud said, he knows where I live, he knows where I work. . . . The guy enjoys butting heads—some sort of macho thing with him, I guess. From my experience, the only way to deal with a guy like that is to confront him head-on. He wins, I give up the pix. He loses, I put him in crap so deep he'll need a snorkel."

Gina fiddled with a lock of her hair for a few minutes, trying to articulate her fears. "The trouble is, you like to butt heads as much as he does. As far as I can see, you two are a pair of cards cut from the same deck. You both make a buck with a camera."

"If I have to explain the difference, I might as well leave right now."

"Sorry. It's just that you're such an easy target sometimes. What do you do now?"

"I think I'll make a special set of prints for our friend."

"But you haven't got the negatives."

I've got a plan, believe it or not."

"Anything I can do?"

"Would you mind being a photographer for a few minutes?" Carver thought for a second, then expanded on the idea. "I can't get around it. I still need my car—and the real negatives, and the enlarger and chemicals on the backseat. You sure you can't pull some strings downtown and get my car out of the pound?"

"Forget it. There's absolutely no way on earth to get that car out of the pound without paying. If you won't accept my loan offer, you'd be better off trying to steal the hundred bucks or some new darkroom equipment. The pound has more security than Chase Manhattan."

Carver reached for the glass tumbler, but it was empty. "I'm sorry, but I'm not taking any more crap from anybody. I'll take care of Brud. I'll take care of Mo. And you can be damned sure I'll take care of my car. Without paying."

"Impossible."

Carver smiled again. "Wanna bet?"

She folded her arms. "Sure. You lose, you turn yourself in."

"And if I win?"

"You get that backrub."

"It's a deal. But you've got to help. First, I want you to shoot a roll of pictures of yours truly. Then I need you to go up to the stationery store at Twelfth and the Bowery—the place that sells legal forms. And see if you can buy me a box of photographic paper."

"Anything else?"

"Well, since you asked . . . Can I borrow your husband's uniform?"

Chapter Thirty

Just past noon, a new police officer left a walk-up on St. Marks Place. His dark blue trousers were an inch too short, his shoes were a half size too small, and his thick brown hair was an inch past regulation.

Nonetheless, the newest of New York's finest passed muster. Near Astor Place, he got a free shoe shine. At the subway stop at Eighth and Broadway, he stepped past the turnstiles without paying his fare. At the end of the subway platform, where even derelicts feared to tread, he forced a trio of young toughs to lower the volume on their boom box.

Ten minutes later, when the RR train finally screeched into the Eighth Street station, the new policeman entered the first car and worked his way through the train as it careened northward. His presence had a salutory effect on the passengers. Two secretaries smiled to themselves when he forced a salesman to extinguish a cigar, and applause broke out when he convinced a teenager with a green Mohawk to surrender his seat to a pregnant shopper.

The novice cop soon realized that whoever said cleanliness was next to godliness was wrong. The next best thing to godliness was being a cop. In fact, many a New York patrolman believed the two were one and the same.

The policeman got off the subway at Times Square and navigated the subterranean maze to the concrete stairs at Seventh Avenue and Forty-second Street. At the traffic light, he rapped on the window of a blue-and-white and called: "Do me a favor, bub. I need a ride to the car pound, Thirty-eighth and Twelfth."

The driver leaned over and unlocked the door.

His passenger introduced himself with a quick handshake: "The name is Carver. Ninth Precinct."

The light changed, and the patrol car headed west past the sorry rows of food stands and porno stores and B-movie marquees. The driver scanned the sidewalks for signs of trouble. As he spoke, his eyes moved slowly from side to side, like windshield wipers: "Your name's familiar. Ever assigned to the Sixth?"

"Can't say I was."

"What brings you up here?" the cop asked, then slowed the patrol car while he checked a shoeless derelict who sat passed out in a doorway.

"You don't want to know," Carver improvised. "I'm on my captain's rag list. Got caught on duty with a hooker holding my nightstick, and now I'm doing gofer work till the departmental hearing."

The driver nodded sympathetically. "That's tough. I was just about to ask where your service revolver was."

"Like I said, let's not talk about it."

"Whatever you say," the cop replied. "What about your face?"

"Tried breaking up a mugging without my gun. But like I said, let's not talk about it. Bad day."

The cop behind the wheel fell silent until the blue-and-white swung left onto Twelfth Avenue, by the Dayliner pier. "Pound's right up ahead."

"Thanks. Just wait for a second till I'm clear."

The patrol car pulled alongside the pound's entrance, a cinder block pillbox with a manual tollgate beside it. A sign announced "PARKING ENFORCEMENT SQUAD TOW-AWAY PROGRAM," and for doubters, several tow-away-zone signs were posted on the chain link fence that secured the area. An air of unease hung over the place, as if the island of Manhattan were Cuba and this spit of land were Guantanamo Bay.

Carver approached the booth and, when the gatekeeper looked up from his worn copy of *Hustler*, Carver signaled the blue-and-white to roll.

The gatekeeper jumped to his feet and opened the door just in time for Carver's KodaChrome smile. "Thanks, officer," Carver told him, "but don't get up. How'd you know I was from Downtown?"

The guard seemed indifferent, but Carver sensed the problem wasn't laziness—for many Traffic Department employees, English was a second language. Carver tried to use that to advantage, waving a fistful of documents and speaking rapidly: "I'm here to retrieve a car. Downtown said they cleared it with you guys. Evidence in a big court case on the docket today. But you don't care about all that."

When the guard realized this wasn't a surprise inspection, he assumed his public servant sneer. "I didn't get no call."

"Yo, bub. Doesn't matter to me if you got the word or not. I'm telling you I'm here to pick up a car, and I got enough paperwork to redecorate the walls of this dump."

The guard asked to see the release forms.

"Hey, first I gotta make sure the car's here, right?" Carver said. "See you in a few minutes."

Fifteen yards away stood the entrance to Pier Seventy-six, a huge aluminum-roofed cinder block building that jutted fifty yards out over the Hudson River.

Pier Seventy-six is a gulag for vehicles seized by the Traffic Department. The crime can range from double parking in Midtown to having out-of-state license plates. Judgment is meted out with Vatican-level infallibility. If you want to see your car again, you surrender your rights at the door and your money at the cashier windows in the information room.

As Carver approached the building, he felt a raw November gust whip off the Hudson, and for warmth he tucked his hands inside the pockets of his police-issue blue nylon jacket. He felt half a roll of Life Savers in the left-hand pocket. When he realized they had belonged to Gina's husband, he decided they were bad luck. He flipped the roll into a metal trash bin and entered the building.

The interior resembled a huge airplane hangar, cavernous and clammy-cold. To the right was a pile of car doors and auto parts. To the left, past the office trailers and the line of police barricades, was the information room. There, motorists waited for an hour or more for the privilege of telling their tales of sorrow and paying their fines. Carver went to that room first, to see if a cashier would tell him where he could find his Rabbit.

Inside, two dozen people stood in line in a room that measured fifteen feet by twenty. It had been painted the color of dried blood, and the linoleum in front of the five cashiers' windows was worn down to bare concrete from the thousands of motorists who'd supplicated there over the years.

Carver ignored the lines and squeezed his way to the front. "Yo, ma'am." He tapped the window grille with his nightstick. "This will only take a second. Here to pick up a car for headquarters. License NYP 555. New York plates."

The cashier ignored him, and he felt obliged to add: "I'm here to take the car or take your name, ma'am. Your choice."

The woman scanned a list on a clipboard. "Zone Two, Area J. That'll be two hundred dollars."

By the time she looked up, he was gone.

The Rabbit was where the clerk said it would be. Aside from a fresh dent in the rear bumper (courtesy of the tow truck's maw, no doubt), the car appeared unscathed. He wiped the dirt from the hatchback window with the fleshy part of his palm. His darkroom gear and the reverse directory were still there. Miracles never ceased.

The Rabbit started on the third wheeze. It was high-strung to begin with, and sitting on the pier over the weekend hadn't helped its disposition. He recognized the malady and prescribed a few minutes of running at idle.

Thirty seconds later, he abandoned that plan. In the rearview mirror, he saw two guards approach. Carver's right foot pushed the accelerator and the left one popped the clutch, and the Rabbit went lurching down the pier. He waved as he drove past the guards and through the open doors. Ten yards from the gatekeeper's booth, the car sputtered twice and quit.

When the gatekeeper stepped outside, he recognized Carver and began to gripe in broken English.

Carver smiled politely and tried to restart the Rabbit. The best it could muster was a cough. He lowered the window and shouted: "I think it's flooded. Give me a minute, and I'll try again."

He glanced in the rearview mirror again. A car had pulled up behind him. He signaled the driver to wait, then tried to restart the Rabbit. The car backfired and bobbed to the tollgate.

The gatekeeper sneezed, wiped his nose on his sleeve, and held out his hand for the paperwork. Carver kept smiling as he presented the documents. The gatekeeper inspected them, then asked: "What is this? Where is the receipt?"

"Let's go, bub. Monday is no-receipt day. This is government business, and I'm late. If you don't let me outta here, I'm gonna make *you* explain to the D.A."

A horn honked, and Carver looked in the rearview again. Three cars were behind him now. The guard hesitated, and Carver pressed his advantage: "Come on, bub. Those drivers behind me are waiting, the judge is waiting, I'm waiting. The city can't possibly be paying you enough to put up with this garbage. Why bother? Let me go. Anybody asks, you give them these papers."

The gatekeeper turned away, spit on the pavement, and then raised the barrier. Carver revved the engine again, shifted into first, and bounded past the raised gate. After hanging a one-eighty, he chugged south on Twelfth Avenue and wondered how long it would take the gatekeeper to notice that the big gold sticker on the front of the documents was courtesy of Publishers Clearing House.

Chapter Thirty-one

On the way to Gina's, Will Carver double-parked by the camera store and retrieved the fresh set of negatives that Gina had dropped off. At an indoor garage on Fourth Avenue, he retrieved the other negatives from under the passenger seat of the Rabbit and removed the orange crate that held the enlarger and chemicals.

He checked his watch: half past two. He had two and a half hours to set up a darkroom at Gina's, pull a dozen prints, and leave them at the drop point by Stuyvesant Square.

Gina met him at the landing in her apartment building. She seemed pleasant, but something was wrong. She was leaning to one side and fiddling with a gold hoop earring. "How did it go?" she asked, and started up the stairs.

"The subway was no picnic. Other than that, it went fine."

"Nobody stopped you?"

"What for? All I did was steal my own car. I never realized how much fun being a cop is."

"Sure, until some nut starts shooting at you."

"I got news for you. Cops haven't cornered the market on gun-toting weirdos. Everybody's in the line of fire."

Gina opened the door and replied, "In that case, you might as well take off Paul's uniform. I imagine you've sullied it enough for one afternoon."

"That's the other great thing about being a cop. Chicks are always asking you to take off your uniform."

"Take a hike."

"Come on, I even got the shoes shined. Don't take everything so serious. You think I liked wearing this outfit? You think I like the fact that you still keep your husband's uniform hanging in your bedroom closet? He's been dead three years. When will you let go?"

"When will you stop prying into other people's business?"

"Forget it. I'm sorry. I was out of line. I'll get changed and get to work. You want to help?"

"I'm sure you're old enough to change by yourself." A trace of a smile crossed her lips, and she took some of the chemicals from the crate and carried them into the bathroom. By the time he changed into his shirt and jeans, she had the trays and enlarger in place.

"How'd you do that so fast?"

"I live above a bookstore, remember? While you were stealing your car, I got a photography book. And the photographic paper. You better mix the chemicals yourself."

Together they finished setting up the trays and tongs. On occasion, they bumped elbows or fannies, and he wondered if Gina needed to be close as much as he did.

After checking the enlarger, he replaced the bulb in the ceiling fixture with an amber safelight, went to the kitchen for a bottle of vinegar, then crammed a towel under the door to block other light.

"Now I've got you right where I want you," Carver said.

"And no room to do anything about it, fortunately," Gina replied. "Just tell me how you plan to give the prints of the dirty pictures to the blackmailers and not play into their hands. It doesn't matter if the negatives you give them are fakes if you give them a set of real prints."

"Easy. When we make these prints, we'll use this vinegar instead of fixer. Vinegar retards the developing process, but it doesn't stop it. If we give these prints a shelf life of a couple of hours, that should get me enough time to go to the transvestite bar and start tracking down the poor sap in the pictures."

Gina was skeptical. "What if the prints turn black sooner?"

"Then Brud and his goon still have to find me. Besides, I can buy some time while they get prints from the phony negatives."

"But why bother with the prints and negatives at all?"

"Because I'm outmanned and outarmed, and I've got to keep

knocking them off balance, keep putting them on the defensive until they screw up enough that I can nail them."

"How do you drop off the film without getting killed?"

"That's the one advantage of having bums for friends. One of my Bowery pals will be glad to drop it off for a bottle of T-bird."

"Okay, so far, but how do you know you won't run into one of the blackmailers at the transvestite bar?"

He rolled his eyes. "You ask enough questions for two cops. I'm going to the bar shortly, and it should be empty except the bartender. It's still afternoon."

"But the bartender . . ."

"I know the guy. Considering that he works in a transvestite bar, he seems fairly straight."

Carver finished the darkroom work by four-thirty and got ready to leave.

Gina walked over, placed a hand on his left shoulder, and asked what more she could do.

"I suggest you stay out of it from here on in," he answered. "I gotta steer clear of this place for a while. You can't risk seeing me again until this is done with."

He expected her to cry, but he should have known better.

Instead, she squeezed his shoulder. "That makes a lot of sense. You know, sometimes I think that underneath it all, you're a decent guy."

"You been watching old movies or something? Don't you believe it for a second."

"And don't you tell me what to do. I can think what I like, and right now I think we have a bet to settle. I owe you a backrub."

He squirmed away. "You were right the first time. You don't want to get involved. I'm too rough around the edges, and I always will be. Don't worry about me."

He walked to the armchair by the front door and put on the flak jacket and his peacoat. "I'll return the jacket later, when I pick up my camera and the darkroom stuff."

She called to him.

"I mean it. I have to go."

"I know," she said. "I was just trying to tell you not to forget your Phillies cap."

He retrieved the cap from the bedroom. A moment later he was gone.

Chapter Thirty-two

Brud Siracusa was pacing his office, waiting for Mo to return with a new set of prints, when he got the call.

Brud extinguished his cigarette in the ashtray, then picked up the phone receiver slowly. He felt a pang of nausea when he recognized the voice.

"Yeah, man, I know the money's due tomorrow night. Relax. You'll get your money. It's in the works now. Trust me." Brud cringed. Saying "Trust me" to a loan shark was like telling him to go screw himself.

Brud waited patiently for the loan shark to finish shouting through the earpiece, then tried to calm him down. "I said not to worry, I'm good for it. Believe me, what I got cooking is as solid as Fort Knox."

Brud patted his coat pocket in hopes of finding a pack of cigarettes, to no avail. "Save your threats. I know what'll happen to me. Don't worry. It's as good as in your wallet now. I promise." Brud hung up quickly, before his caller could make the threats more specific—Brud had already gotten the point.

This was no time to sweat the debt, Brud decided. At least now there was light at the end of the sewer. Mo had already dropped off the set of blackmail photos, and at that very moment Mo would be up on Eighth Street at a one-hour film lab getting another set of prints from the negatives. Brud picked up the manila envelope and, for reassurance, slid out the set of prints that Carver had left on the steps to the church on Stuyvesant Square.

Brud looked at the prints again, and his face went white. Every exposure had gone solid black.

Before the shock had set in, the phone rang again. This time it was Mo: The woman at the photography store had just asked him why he needed a dozen eight-by-ten glossies of some guy in a Phillies cap giving him the finger.

Chapter Thirty-three

About five-fifteen P.M., Will Carver walked into Acey-Deucey's on Bleecker Street. The place was so empty that he thought for a second the West Village had gone straight.

By Manhattan standards, Acey's was your basic bar. Big bay window facing the street, hanging plants, brass footrails along the oak bar, ceiling fans, and a floor done in white tiles the size and shape of Oysterette crackers. An old pinball machine, "High Ace," on the far wall next to the jukebox.

The only signs that the place might have a different kind of clientele were the pink front doors, the photos on the wall (eight-by-ten glossies of Milton Berle, Flip Wilson, Mae West, and scenes from *Some Like It Hot*), and the signs over the two rest rooms. They were marked "LADIES" and "WOMEN."

Carver walked to the middle of the twenty-foot-long bar and waved to the barkeep, who stood at a pay phone with his back to the front entrance.

"Hey, Tracey, where is everybody? Falsies on sale at Bloomies or what?"

Tracey muttered something, then quickly hung up the phone. Looking flustered, he primped his hair and brushed some imaginary dandruff off the shoulder of his lime green jumpsuit. Then he strolled behind the bar, wiped the stretch of counter between Carver and himself and poured a draft of Beck's Dark.

"Don't get your bowels in an uproar, love," Tracey said. "It's still afternoon. You know the regulars don't roll in till after five-thirty or so. Hell, it takes them a good hour or so to change and put on their makeup."

134

Tracey spoke in a nervous whisper so delicate that it sounded like he'd talcum-powdered his throat. The voice wasn't exactly effeminate in itself, but the rest of Tracey's act left that impression. His teased, shoulder-length hair was strawberry blond today and brushed to a fare-thee-well. The eyebrows smacked of makeup.

In the three years Carver had been coming here, he could never decide what the story with Tracey was. He suspected a sex-change operation at work but couldn't determine the direction.

Furthermore, he didn't care. He liked Tracey, in small doses at least, and he liked the bar. Aside from the strong scent of Chanel and a lot of cackling over wardrobes, Acey-Deucey's was a comfortable place, and the patrons didn't mind having their pictures taken. Ever since he'd learned how to push Tri-X in the darkroom so he could shoot in low light, Carver didn't need to use a strobe unit, which had made some patrons edgy. And he gave his subjects free prints of their best poses.

When Carver had first started frequenting Acey-Deucey's in search of subjects, he expected a tough time shooting the transvestites. It proved the contrary. As one transvestite once confided: "There are only two things we can't live without—a mirror and a camera."

The reason was simple. After spending all that time preening, shaving, applying makeup, and shoehorning themselves into their Lane Bryant outfits, the patrons needed to get their pictures taken: confirmation in black and white that they were as attractive as their blouses and spangled sweater vests.

"Tracey, I need your help."

"How's that?"

Carver reached into his pocket for a photograph and flipped it onto the bar. "I was wondering if you remember this person. I think I took the picture here. See the movie poster in the background? Sure looks like this joint."

Tracey pushed the picture away. "Go suck a lemon. You know the rules. No personal questions, no real names, no prying, no publicity."

"You haven't even looked at the picture yet." Carver turned

the photo so Tracey could sneak a look, but Tracey was glancing toward the phone. "What would make it worth your while?"

Tracey rolled his eyes, feigning indignation.

"Come on, Tracey. What if I said you'd be doing this person a big favor?"

Tracey fluttered like a frightened sparrow. "I can't. Really."

Then he abruptly changed his mind. "One hundred bucks, love, and I give the person the message—you can't contact the person directly. That's assuming, of course, that I've made this person's acquaintance."

"I don't care if you've made the guy himself. What I'm saying here is this sweetheart doesn't know it, but he has his butt in a wringer. You can help him get it out. Problem is, I only got fifty bucks I can spare."

Carver put the money on the bar. Money always talked louder when it was out in the open.

Tracey picked up the photo and held it so it caught the overhead light just right. Carver sensed that Tracey was stalling.

Finally, Tracey put the photo on the counter. "That just won't do, love. I'm not saying I know this person, or that this person has been in this establishment. I'm saying if this person comes in sometime, I'll relay your message—for a hundred dollars. Fifty dollars won't keep me in rouge. Besides, how do I know you're not trying to blackmail this fair person? I wouldn't want to be a party to that."

"Come on, Tracey, how long have you known me? Four years? You know I'm the straightest arrow that ever walked through your pink doors. Like I said, I'm trying to help your friend. If I wanted to blackmail him, you think I'd get anyone else involved?"

"Tell you what, love," Tracey replied with a twitter of mascara. "I'll take the fifty dollars here as a down payment. You come back with the other fifty in an hour or so. A man of your means, you have resources, no?"

"Save your sweet talk for your other customers," Carver replied, but he knew he was losing the battle. "Okay. You're on, but I need the fifty to prime the pump. I'm going to do myself a little gambling on Eighth Street and see if I can't scrape up some more money. Meanwhile, save us some time and tell your pal I'll give him a buzz here at nine tonight. Trust me. I'll be back with your dough."

Carver finished the last of his beer, tossed a few dollars on the bar, and pushed through the swinging doors. He headed east on Bleecker, past the empty storefront restaurants and the cluttered windows of the antiques shops. If he had to make some fast money, Eighth Street would be the place—lots of tourists ready to throw their money away and not many cops to stop them.

Chapter Thirty-four

"I'll bet you any amount of money you can't find the queen. Who's next? Who's next?"

On the southeast corner of Eighth Street and Sixth Avenue, a three-card monte dealer was trying to drum up business, and Will Carver was doing his best to scout the operation discreetly. Carver took a deep breath: There was no harder way to make a buck than to cheat a crook or sue a lawyer. He held both groups in equal esteem.

Actually, he figured he had a decent chance of winning at three-card monte. He'd watched enough games to know how. The trouble with going up against a three-card monte operation was that even if you won you'd probably lose. The dealer's confederates had a habit of mugging you as soon as you left with your winnings.

Their preferred means of persuasion were long screwdrivers with sharpened points—Carver called them "ghetto stilettos"—and they seldom left any doubt who was getting screwed.

Three-card monte is a variation of the old shell game: The hand is quicker than the eye. On a makeshift table, the dealer places three cards, the two red tens and the queen of spades—bent in half lengthwise. He shows which of the three cards is the queen, mixes the cards several times, then bets you can't guess where the queen is: Now you see it, now you lose.

To beat the dealer, you have to stay one step ahead of him. In addition to knowing which card is the queen after the three cards have been deftly rearranged, you'd better know who the lookouts are, who the shill is, and when they're setting up a sucker for a fall.

What amazed Carver was that the game was still around. Hucksters had plied it on the streets of Manhattan for more than two decades, yet there always seemed to be a new batch of fools who insisted on parting with their money.

Carver figured he wouldn't be the next chump to pad this operation's bankroll. After a minute or two, he walked back down Sixth Avenue. He hailed a cab, gave the driver two dollars, and told him to start the meter—Carver'd signal from the end of the block when he was ready to roll

As he walked back to the corner, he heard the dealer continue his spiel: "All right, everybody, check out the best deal in the Big Apple. Before me I have three cards, slightly bent so as to be totally indistinguishable. Find the queen. Be a king."

The speaker stood five-foot-six. He had a pasty complexion, a green-and-red watch cap atop his head, and an unlit cigarette that flapped from his lips as he spoke. "I mix the cards. Two tens and a queen. You guess where the little lady went, and you double your dough. Easy money. Who's next? Who's next?"

A young Pakistani in a business suit stepped forward and produced a small roll of bills. That must be the shill, Carver decided. The question was, which scam would they work? The hype or the dog ear? It didn't take long to find out.

"Aw right, my good man, what do you wager?" As the dealer spoke, he tossed the cards, three in a row. Then he scooped them up and flipped them onto the cardboard box again.

Mr. Businessman smiled, tucked his parcel under his left arm, and peeled a twenty off the top of his roll. The dealer shuffled the cards once more and laid them facedown on the table. Mr. Businessman pointed to the middle card. It was a ten of diamonds. He was down twenty dollars.

"Let's go. Try again. Twenty will get you forty."

The dealing continued. Mr. Businessman seemed deep in concentration, furrowing his brows and then putting his finger on the third card that landed on the makeshift table. He produced another crisp twenty-dollar bill.

Wrong again.

"Hey, buddy, you must be cheating," claimed Mr. Businessman. He picked up the ten of diamonds in disgust and flicked it to the pavement.

As the dealer knelt to retrieve the card, the Pakistani reached out and bent a corner on the queen ever so gingerly. The dealer stood and shuffled the cards again. He didn't seem to notice the bent card.

Another deal, and to no one's surprise Mr. Businessman won twenty dollars. The bent card was easy to detect if you knew to look for it. After the next shuffle, he doubled his bet to forty dollars—and suddenly he was up twenty dollars.

The dealer acted frazzled, and the small cluster of spectators sensed that for once the dealer was the one getting snookered: He still hadn't noticed the bent corner on the queen.

When the Pakistani took him for another forty dollars, the dealer refused to continue. "Beat it, buddy. You doin' somethin' funny here. Give someone else a chance. Let's go."

He turned to Carver. "How about you, my man? Ten will get you twenty. Find the queen and be a hero. Just show your dough."

Carver glanced at the cards. The queen was still bent. He nodded yes to the dealer.

The dealer started mixing the cards two at a time, then flicked the bent card down in the middle and the last card to the right.

"Will you go fifty?" Carver inquired.

The dealer grinned a grin so wide that the cigarette almost fell out of his mouth. "It's your money, my good man. Any amount you want to wager is copacetic with me."

"Then put your fifty on the table on top of mine."

"Well, well. This gent doesn't trust me, folks," the dealer said. Then he poked into his pants pocket, found two twenties and a ten, and slapped them down on Carver's wager.

With that, Carver reached past the bent card and upended the one to its right.

The trick never failed. Every time a three-card monte dealer tried the bent-card ploy, you could bet the last card dealt would be your queen.

As Carver reached for his money, a hand grabbed his wrist.

For an instant, Carver considered making a run for his waiting cab. A gun poking against his kidney changed his mind.

"All right, boys, your fun is over," boomed the voice from over Carver's shoulder. "Plainclothes. I'll take the money. Evidence. Sir, you'll have to come with me and fill out a statement."

Carver turned to see a man about his height, with rust-colored hair, a pockmarked face, and a neck that was still red from the picture-hanging wire.

Chapter Thirty-five

The moon was a ten-watt bulb on the horizon as two men walked eastward past commuters and tourists along Eighth Street. You couldn't tell that one man had a gun in his pocket, aimed at the other man's back.

Will Carver was well aware of the gun, however, and he knew he had to weigh the options fast. Should he try to jump Mo, make a run for it, or keep stalling until he could think of something that might save his hide? Unfortunately, long about now he was out of patience and a quart low on finesse.

"Hey, Mo. I forgot to tell you this morning. You broke my rat trap, and you really should reimburse me."

"Stow it," Mo replied calmly. "Mr. Siracusa wants to have a chat with you, but first we're going to reach a little understanding. Turn right at the corner."

"Where are we going—Washington Square?" Carver asked. "That place isn't safe after dark, not even for scum like you."

When they turned the corner, Mo pointed to a building across the street. "How about over there?"

Carver turned to look—and should have known better. He never saw the kick coming. It landed flush to the groin, and it had the force of a shovel. Carver crumpled to the sidewalk and curled into a ball.

"In case you hadn't figured out by now, I like nailing wise alecks like you. I got your negatives developed: pictures of some ugly asswipe in a Phillies cap giving the finger. Real cute. The other pictures you gave us turned black. We're through messing around. Now get up and walk into the park."

Carver tried to regain his balance. He stumbled instead, once again hiking his elbows to fend off any more shots. Mo just stood there.

"I gotta sit," Carver said.

"In the park. Let's go."

They found a bench to the right of the arch in Washington Square, and Carver plopped down, still trying to get his senses back. His groin was on fire from the kick, and he couldn't get his breath back.

"Where's the real film?" Mo asked.

"I don't have it."

"I guess I have to knock some sense into you," Mo replied.

And he did, with a crisp right to the side of Carver's head.

Carver collapsed on the bench, waiting for the next punch. His ears were ringing so much from the punch that he barely heard a voice say to his assailant: "Try that again and I blow your brains out. Now give my main man here your gun. Real slow."

As Carver tried to sit upright, he could see a pair of high-topped black sneakers. The brand name had worn off, but they had Puma written all over them, and Carver's spirits lifted.

Once Carver could breathe again, he said: "I see you got your gun back from your mother, Puma. What brings you to Washington Square?"

"What brings you to hustle my associate in his own monte game?" Puma replied. "And what you wanna do with this trash?"

Carver started to wipe the blood from his ear with the sleeve of his peacoat, but the rough wool against the raw flesh made him wince.

"Give me a minute to get my head straight, would you?" Carver said, then paused again to catch his breath. "I can handle this slimeball myself now. He and I have some talking to do."

"Sounds cool. But first he owes me the hundred bucks from the monte game."

Carver interrupted. "Now that you mention it, Mo here owes me three hundred bucks for some lenses he broke."

When Puma cocked the trigger, Mo reached into the hip pocket of his jeans and handed his wallet to Carver. Carver peeled off four fifties and five twenties for himself, then five twenties for

Puma. "You shouldn't carry so much cash in the Village, Mo," Carver said. He handed the money to Puma.

In the instant Puma looked down to take hold of the money, Mo lunged for the gun. He died instantly.

Chapter Thirty-six

Brud Siracusa sat in his office and cleaned his fingernails with a switchblade while he waited for Mo to arrive with Carver. By now, he was getting fed up—with Carver, with Mo, with the whole stinking deal.

He realized now that sending Mo after Carver had been a mistake. When Tracey blurted that Carver had walked in the door, Brud should have gone after the photographer himself, put the screws to the photographer, not counted on Mo to do the job.

When Brud had finally encountered Carver that morning, he knew in seconds the guy would be a problem: You can't intimidate someone who doesn't give a rat's ass.

Brud thought his orders to Mo had been explicit. Find Carver on Eighth Street and bring him here. No gunplay. On the way, ignore whatever Carver had to say—the guy worked for a newspaper and couldn't be trusted.

Brud looked at his watch. Forty-five minutes had gone by. He tried to picture what was happening this very moment and didn't like the prospects. He loosened his skinny black tie, then opened his gold cigarette case. He had one smoke left. He thought about saving it for later, then changed his mind. The ashtray on the desk brimmed.

If things had gone according to plan, Mo would've returned with Carver already, and they'd be having another little chat—this time on Brud's turf. Now two possibilities loomed. Mo, still smarting from the rat trap episode and the wire noose, lost his cool and shot Carver, and Brud could kiss the film and the quarter-million bucks good-bye.

Brud didn't want to think about the other possibility—that Carver somehow had gotten the upper hand.

Brud started going through his desk drawers in hopes of coming across an extra pack of cigarettes, then started roaming the room. Finally, on the bookshelf by the door, he found a somewhat flattened pack. He peeled back the foil and shook out the last smoke. He considered slipping out to a drugstore to replenish his supply, but he was stuck. What if Mo returned and Brud were gone? Mo would probably call the cops.

The phone's ring brought Brud back to matters at hand. It was his partner.

"What do you mean Mo's dead?"

Brud felt a chill and reached for his jacket. "When? Where? How?"

Somehow, the news wasn't a surprise: Mo had been bushwhacked in Washington Square, and the cops had found a phone number for Acey-Deucey's in Mo's pants pocket. A bystander had given them descriptions of the assailants, Tracey said. It had to be the fat black kid and Carver.

"The cops catch them yet? . . . Yeah, that figures. Well, think of it as a pure two-way split now. . . . No way. How's Carver going to find our sweetheart? . . . And there's no way he's going to the cops. I'll take care of him tomorrow, and that's all there is to it. Good night."

Brud walked over to the punching bag, rolled up his shirtsleeves, and pummeled the leather till his knuckles ached.

When he'd calmed down enough to think rationally, Brud returned to his desk, retracted the blade on his knife, and slid it into his pants pocket. Next, he opened the bottom drawer. From a cigar box, he extracted his revolver and six hollow-point bullets.

Chapter Thirty-seven

Propped against the bar at McSorley's, Will Carver felt like death eating an onion. In spite of three mugs of ale and four aspirins, his face throbbed so much he thought it would burst. He was tired. His back was acting up. His groin hurt. He had nowhere to go, no one to turn to. And Brud was probably out looking to kill him at this very moment.

As for the cops, they didn't have much to go on if they tried to connect him to Mo's death. As far as Carver could remember, nobody in Washington Square had been close enough to get a good look at him or Puma, and the cops probably wrote off the slaying as a sloppy mugging or an amateurish drug transaction. Even if they traced the slaying to Puma and him, Carver couldn't find much of a crime to charge them with. The bottom line was that Puma had stepped in to save Carver's life, and Carver certainly had the lumps to prove it. The only mistake had been to take Mo's money, even if it had settled old accounts.

The bartender, an Irishman just off the boat, didn't help improve Carter's spirits by telling him he looked like the guy who lost the chariot race to Ben Hur in the old Charlton Heston flick. Yeah, Carver agreed, but at least the guy in the movie had had the good sense to die and put himself out of his misery.

Carver didn't say it as though he were joking, so the bartender dumped the ashtray and moved down the bar, leaving Carver to mope in solitude.

Something else bothered Carver, and he finally realized what it was: When Puma had pulled the trigger and plugged Mo smackdab in the middle of his forehead, Carver's reaction wasn't fear, repulsion, or even sadness. Carver had felt anger: He didn't have a camera with him, and he was missing a chance for a great shot. No matter how hard he tried to suppress them, old instincts died hard.

On the positive side, he did have three hundred dollars in his back pocket, and he allowed himself a small smile: Going from death's door to a semiwealthy man in a matter of minutes constituted a small turn of fortune. Maybe Puma got his nickname for the way he pounced after all.

After the shooting, Puma had bolted in the direction of SoHo and Carver headed toward the East Village. Carver's first impulse had been to go to Gina's and apply an icepack to the side of his head, but he knew he had to leave her out of this.

Instead, he stopped for cigars and headed to McSorley's on East Seventh. In the bad old days, when Carver's marriage had disintegrated and he'd lost his drive, he always came here to lose himself. Ever since, when he had some serious thinking to do, he headed for McSorley's. The ale was cheap and the customers usually minded their own business—except on weekends, when tourists and drunken college kids took over the joint.

In the early seventies, McSorley's was an ale house *célèbre*. It was the last all-male bar in New York, and almost every week some new batch of feminists crashed the place in an effort to break the sex barrier. At the time, Carver had thought the women were grandstanding. After all, what woman in her right mind would want to go to a dumpy old East Village bar that served nothing but ale—and side orders of cheese, sweet onions, and crackers. No jukebox, no Muzak, no tablecloths, no flowers, no couth: Carver heaven. Now that women frequented the place, it had become almost respectable.

Carver leaned on the bar and rubbed his index finger around the rim of the thick six-ounce mug. He wondered where he could turn, but he kept coming up empty. His apartment would be like the Little Big Horn. He considered spending the night at the station house a couple of blocks away, then remembered that there was an outside chance the police were looking for him. But even if they weren't, he now understood how awkward things had gotten over there—and how far apart he and Joe Gold had drifted in the past few years. Joe was brass now, and knowing Carver could only tarnish him.

First chance, he'd stop by the station house and clear out his belongings. The time had come to move on.

Thinking about Joe, Carver realized it had been time to move on years ago—not just from the station house but from his days as a street photographer. Joe was getting ahead in the world. Carver was going at an Indy 500 pace, driving in an endless circle.

As he stood at the bar, nursing the mugs of ale, he concluded that the past few years of his life had been . . . He groped for the right word. The past few years had been like the times he'd be driving along so wrapped up in the events of the day he couldn't remember whether the traffic lights had been green or red—he couldn't even remember going through the intersections.

What if, through some minor miracle, he managed to walk away from this huge, mucked-up disaster? Go back to recording life's tragedies on thirty-five-millimeter film? It was a younger man's game, if it was a game at all. Carver couldn't tell anymore.

Once upon a time, Carver had steadfastly believed that if the pen were mightier than the sword, then the camera had come to be mightier than the pen. After all, what did the most to end America's involvement in Vietnam—the countless articles and TV reports from the front lines or a handful of photographs that brought home the horrors of war?

Newspaper and magazine articles about the war were but ripples in a sea of words that readers scanned everyday, and TV news coverage was a series of fleeting images diluted by commercials. But a few stark photographs—of a South Vietnamese brigadier general shooting a prisoner in the head at point-blank range, of a screaming Vietnamese girl running naked from a napalm attack—never could be forgotten.

Whenever someone called Carver's pictures splatter shots, he gave a similar defense. He took the pictures he did because they made people look at situations they'd spent their lives trying to ignore—derelicts sleeping in their own urine puddles, women grieving over their slain husbands, battered wives bleeding in emergency wards.

Tonight, as thoughts of Bingo's sister and the jumper's father flickered in and out of his mind, he understood how threadbare his justifications were. In truth, the people who paid their thirty-five cents to buy the *News* and look at his photos enjoyed what they saw—a cheap glimpse at a freak show, a front-row seat at a head-on collision.

They'd put down the paper, eat breakfast on their oiled butcher-block tables, and go about their go-to-church-on-Easter lives. If things weren't going swimmingly, they could look at the pictures and sigh: There but for the grace of God goes my brother-in-law.

Carver used to think he was their conscience. Now, he finally understood, he was nothing more than their sometime tour guide to Manhattan's underbelly.

What was the difference between his photographs and the pictures some poor freak was about to be blackmailed for? Maybe a hundred thousand people saw one of Carver's pictures on the front page and paid thirty-five cents for a closer look. In the other case, one person probably would have to pay a few hundred grand so others would never get that chance.

Either way, it was blood money.

Chapter Thirty-eight

Lieutenant Joe Gold frisked himself by the front entrance to the Ninth Precinct station house.

As usual, he'd misplaced his car keys. It was eleven P.M., Gold had an hour's drive to his house upstate, and the next-to-last thing he needed was lost keys.

The last thing he needed was Gina Constantine approaching him and asking if they could talk.

"Can't it wait, Gina?" He pointed to his wristwatch. "It's been a long night; I've got a long drive. I know your hours could be better, but I don't have any say in that."

"It's about Will Carver."

Joe postponed the search for his car keys and led Gina to the radio room, an oversized closet behind the main desk. The room had no radio, just gray storage lockers for guns. Joe Gold sat on a beat-up metal desk that had cigarette stains along the edges. As he waited for Gina to speak, he idly ran his fingers along the scorch marks. She sat in a steel desk chair a few feet away. She held a steno notebook as if she were about to take dictation.

"What can you tell me about Will Carver?"

Joe groaned. "Please don't say you're seeing that guy." He started to explain his reservations about Carver but caught himself. She had to be seeing him—otherwise why would she ask—and there was no point saying things she wouldn't listen to. Or it could be that Carver was using Gina to pump him for information—Gold wouldn't put it past Carver. "Is this just between you and me? My comments go no further?"

Gina's mouth dropped open. "Yes, it's just between you and me. Why? What do you know?"

"I hate to avoid your question, Gina, but what do I know about what? Him, or his current situation?" Joe looked at his watch again. "Can't this hold?"

"Look, I have to go on duty in a few minutes. Give me that much time."

"Okay, but you still haven't answered my question: Are you seeing Carver?"

"No," Gina replied, which was the truth, sort of. "Not that it's any of your business if I were."

"Then why ask me about him? Never mind. Let's stop ducking each other. What do I think of Carver? I know he's a damned good photographer, although I sometimes don't care for his subject matter. On a personal level, I think he's basically a decent guy, but I couldn't swear to it. I wouldn't say he's crazy, but. . . ."

Joe fumbled for a diplomatic way to say it. "Let's just say he's on a different wavelength from most people. New York's full of oddballs like him. They just don't stick out like they would anywhere else. Does this make sense?"

Gina nodded yes, then added: "Has he always been like this?"

"Like what?"

"You know what I'm getting at—insulated, cynical, afraid of his emotions?"

The desk sergeant tapped on the half-open door and stepped into the room. "Sorry to interrupt, Captain, but your wife's on the phone. Wants to know when to expect you."

Gold looked at Gina and said, "Told you I had to be going. Thanks, Mike, tell her I'll be home in an hour, an hour and a half."

As the sergeant left, Gold called after him. "Mike, you better be wearing your bulletproof vest by the time I leave. You know what happened to Alvarez last Monday night."

Gina remembered the incident. A guy had come in to complain about the way the police had handled a domestic dispute, and when Alvarez didn't tell him what he wanted to hear, he became so exasperated that he pulled out a gun and plugged Alvarez in the chest. Broke a rib, even with the Kevlar body armor.

Gold asked Gina again if she really had to talk now, and when she nodded, he took off his blue jacket and placed it beside him on the desk. He fumbled for a way to begin. "I'm not sure you really want to know all the dirty details about Carver, and I'm not even sure that they're actually the reason he is the way he is."

"Let me decide. Tell me everything."

Gold tugged on his ear, a nervous habit that Gina had seen when Gold was under stress. "How about if I just tell you about his marriage and let you draw your own conclusions? His wife's name was Sandra. Her name still is, in fact. Nice woman, although you'd never get Carver to agree.

"They met while Carver was some sort of darkroom assistant at the *News*. She was a photo stylist—somebody who got paid to arrange the parsley on studio shots, or make sure a model's slip wasn't showing on a fashion shoot.

"After Carver got his big break—he had exclusive shots of some mob hit, as I recall—he suddenly became a hot property. Shot *Time* magazine covers and spreads for *Vogue*, the whole nine yards. Sandra was pretty and all of a sudden she was pretty interested. Carver fell for her. They didn't waste time getting married. . . .

"I guess the crush wore off soon enough. Carver was doing the celebrity bit—everybody wanted to rub elbows with this hotshot crime photographer—and he got so caught up in the Weegee mystique that I guess he didn't give her enough attention anymore, if you get what I'm aiming at. Not a sexual thing, I don't think, but I think Sandra needed to be the center of things, needed to be spoiled.

"So, in a nutshell, because I really gotta head out: Carver's cruising around in his beat-up Studebaker one night, listening to his police radio like he always did, and he hears about this big hotel fire down by Gramercy Park. So he zips down there and arrives the same time as the fire trucks. He grabs two cameras and starts firing away—at the flames curling out the windows, at the firemen, at the guests in various stages of undress as they fell through the main door.

"When Carver gets enough good material, he drives uptown,

puts the film though the soup, and goes over the negatives until he figures he's got a winner—a woman in nothing but a hand towel rushing through the front entrance. You guessed it. Good ol' Sandra.

"So Carver did what any red-blooded photographer would. He hadn't let his marriage interfere with his job before . . ."

Gina was shaking her head no.

"That's right. He submitted that picture, and the *News* ran it on the front page the next day.

"When he got home the next morning, she was at work, and he threw all of her clothes in the hall and changed the lock. Apparently the next and last time he saw her was in court.

"I asked him a while back what happened to her, and know what he said? He said he checks for her picture on the front page of the tabloids, and since he hasn't seen her, he figures she must be frequenting better hotels these days."

Gina frowned. "And that's supposed to excuse his hardass behavior now?"

"Let's just say that it was an easy thing to fall back on, and it got to be a habit. I guess my point is this: I'm not going to ask you again if you're seeing Carver, because your husband was my friend, and I don't want to know about your personal life. . . . But if you're thinking of taking Carver under your wing and trying to reform him or something, I'd suggest you think twice. It's awkward for me to say this, because Carver considers me a pal. But I don't think he'll let anybody get too close, not even you. He's too wrapped up in himself, in his photos. He's tough to get a bead on."

Gina sat there, depressed. Joe hadn't said anything about Carver's behavior she didn't already know, and the time had come for him to leave. "What about now?" she asked. "What's Will mixed up in?"

Joe Gold tugged on his ear again and stared off into space, as though he were deep in thought. "Wish I knew. From all I can gather, he's got himself involved in some pretty heavy heat, and he's in over his head. People are getting killed. Next time you run into him, tell him to level with me. I can help."

Joe reached into his coat pocket for his car keys but still couldn't find them. Then he stood and started for the door.

"Thanks, Joe, but you might better tell him yourself," Gina called after him. "I don't plan on seeing him anytime soon."

Chapter Thirty-nine

By eleven P.M., the area around Avenue B at Fifth Street had become a ghost town. Resembling an urban tumbleweed, an empty beer can rattled along the pavement as an insistent cold wind swept up the avenue from the south. In the gutter, a puddle left from the weekend rains had coagulated into slush.

Across the skinny avenue, the spectre of a brownbagger huddled with his bottle in a sealed-off doorway to P.S. 60, a massive brick fortress that ran from Fourth Street to Sixth Street.

Every first-floor window was secured by iron bars or a grating, and the only signs that the building was an elementary school were the construction paper maple leaves Scotch-taped to the third-floor windows.

Brud Siracusa buried his hands in his overcoat as he approached the area. When he reached the meeting place, a jaundiced yellow-brick nursing home on the corner, he turned so his back would take the brunt of the wind, but it provided little comfort. Nothing could stop the cold from sneaking through the thin leather soles of his loafers and taking the life from his feet. And nothing could stop his paranoia from telling him that this showdown with Puma was ill conceived.

He knew that after dark the area became Beirut West and that he provided an easy target for anyone with an appetite for violence and a craving for crack cocaine. He cradled the handle of his pistol for comfort and prayed Puma would arrive before long.

The Good Lord had invented taxicabs for this kind of weather, but no cabs were to be found along this godless stretch of Manhattan, and he could ill afford to have taken one there anyway, for more reasons than one. This was a business trip that demanded anonymity. All he needed was a cabbie who could place him in the area and pick him out of a police lineup.

Brud shivered. Like a top that had lost its center of gravity, his tightly wound little world was spinning out of control. Mo was dead, the blackmail photos were no closer to his grasp, and the loan shark's deadline was less than twenty-four hours away.

As usual, Tracey had provided the voice of reason earlier that evening: The situation was out of control, but not out of reach. The only way out was clear enough, and Brud rehearsed it again for reassurance as he scouted the terrain for signs of Puma. The blackmail scheme had already been set into motion, and all Tracey and Brud could do was to see it through. A phone call to Stanten confirmed that their blackmailee was trying to scrape up the cash by the appointed deadline, and as Tracey pointed out, Stanten had no choice but to show up at Acey-Deucey's with the money whether they were bluffing or not. If Brud could retrieve the photos by then, they'd make the swap and their problems would be over. If Brud couldn't wrest the photos away from Carver, Brud would have to mug Stanten when he arrived at the bar.

Between now and then, Brud had to tie up the loose ends—Puma and Carver. Tonight he would take care of the fat boy. Tomorrow morning he'd set up for a final confrontation with Carver. Life was only as complicated as you allowed it to be, his mother used to say, and now Brud was bent on simplification.

His one bit of good fortune had been contacting Puma—his family was in the phone book, for heaven's sake—and letting money talk. Brud had sung the praises of a mutually beneficial deal (to the tune of a thousand dollars) and said to be at the corner of East Fifth and Avenue B at eleven. What, Brud had argued, did Puma have to lose by listening to the plan?

Brud hadn't expected Puma to be punctual, but it was now ten after the hour and Brud's knuckles stung so much from the cold that he worried that he wouldn't be able to pull the trigger. Brud watched distractedly as a drunk with a fresh six-pack staggered out of the all-night deli on the other side of Fifth Street.

A tap on the shoulder spun Brud around. Puma towered over him. "Lookin' for me?"

"You nearly scared me to death. How's a man your size sneak around like that?" Brud blurted.

The corners of the big man's lips curled upward, and he nodded knowingly toward his untied high tops. He looked again at Brud and caught the glint of the revolver.

Brud spoke next. "Like the song goes, walk this way."

Chapter Forty

Silence reigned in the newsroom at the *Daily News*. It was midnight and the place was deserted, save for a few editors on hand to remake a page or two in the event of a late-breaking tragedy.

Tomorrow morning's editions had already been beamed to satellite printing presses in the suburbs, and webs of pages now rolled off the presses to be cut, folded, stacked, and delivered to newsstands and payboxes within a hundred-mile radius of Manhattan.

Will Carver roamed the seventh floor in hopes of finding something to take his mind off Mo and the confrontation in Washington Square. On impulse, he walked into Ralph's office and looked to see if any paychecks might await him. Nothing. He opened a desk drawer and found a business envelope. He addressed the envelope to a woman in Upper Darby, Pennsylvania, and wrote his name above the **News**'s return address. He then counted two hundred dollars in fifties and twenties, slid them into the envelope, and licked it shut.

Over the past decade, Carver had repeated the ritual dozens of times—whenever he had money to spare. The money never came back, nor was it acknowledged.

As he placed the envelope in the bin for outgoing mail, he wondered if this would be the last time and if he should have included some sort of farewell. But then he'd never really said hello.

He had only the gauziest recollection of his mother. She'd placed him in a boarding school when he was three and, save for an occasional letter with no return address, had cut all contact.

He'd saved her letters—still had them bundled in a dresser drawer—but the answers they contained seemed inadequate. She'd written that she'd met his father when he was stationed in Philly. She worked as a waitress at a luncheonette near the navy yard, and he used to stop by on his days off. They wed the day before he shipped out. Her parents had disapproved and disowned her.

She was six months pregnant when she learned he died in an accident during maneuvers on an aircraft carrier somewhere in the Pacific. She was twenty-two at the time and couldn't support herself and care for a young child. So when he was three, she reluctantly enrolled him in a school for fatherless boys and tried to start fresh.

By the time Carver was old enough to understand, she was beyond reach. Ever since, he'd yearned to see her and ask about his father. Only once had he gotten the chance.

It came the summer his marriage crumbled, and Carver had found himself adrift—sleeping till noon and missing assignments, quitting early and drinking late. To find out where he was headed, he decided to find his mother and reestablish some sort of bond.

After postponing the trip a few times out of a combination of dread and inertia, he finally packed a knapsack, walked to Penn Station, and caught the next train for Philly. He checked into a run-down hotel northeast of City Hall and went out for a six-pack. It was too muggy to do much else.

The next morning, the first of September, Carver washed and shaved and headed to the boarding school. At the records office, he cajoled a clerk into letting him look at his file. There wasn't much to go on, but he wrote down what information he could find. The last entry was from sixty-nine, the year he graduated. The last record of his mother was three years before that. The address had been lost.

Next stop was the public library, where he combed through the area phone books until he came across an entry for an Agnes Carver in Upper Darby. He wrote the address in his notepad and added a question mark.

Late that afternoon, he checked out of the hotel, lifted his knapsack onto his shoulder, and took the elevated train from center city to Sixty-ninth Street. At the terminal, he asked where her street was, then strode past the rows of stores up the steep hill to Gimbel's. The heat wave had finally broken, and Carver found a bounce returning to his step.

He crossed the street at the traffic light, walked past the parking lot and down a slight incline. At the next intersection, he began to check the address in the notepad against the numbers on the brick row homes. The one in question was third from the corner. Without thinking what he would say, Carver climbed eight concrete steps to the screen aluminum door and rang the bell.

No answer.

It was getting on toward six P.M., and the first scents of autumn floated in the air, a blend of cut grass and the first fallen leaves. Down the block, two ten-year-old boys in green Eagles jerseys tossed a football in the street, pausing by the curb every so often as a car crept past.

Carver wondered what it would have been like to grow up here instead of center city, wondered whether he'd have turned out different, better. And what would she think of him now? He decided it was tough to become a man your mother would be proud of when you never knew what her expectations were.

But what ate at him more was what he would think of her. Would he see himself in her? Why had she abandoned him? He concluded that it was too late to make a difference. She'd had her reasons, and when you got right down to it, they didn't matter anymore.

Carver stood daydreaming on the steps until he heard the two boys' mother call them for dinner, saw them race up their front steps three at a time, saw the door close behind them and the porch light flick on. The knapsack felt heavy. Time to go. He'd take the el back to the Thirtieth Street station and catch a train to Manhattan.

As Carver walked up the slight rise toward Sixty-ninth Street, he saw a woman in her late forties approaching on the other side of the street. She was about five-foot-four, medium build, square face framed by dusty brown hair. She wore a pale blue dress with a white cardigan sweater, pearl earrings, and sensible shoes.

He stopped and watched her walk by. She looked past him, as

though he didn't exist. Carver picked up his stride again and didn't glance back—afraid to see which house she entered.

Later, as the train clacked through the no-man's-land of central Jersey, Carver gazed out the window. Whenever a farmhouse flew past, he stole a look through the house's lighted windows, then tried to imagine who lived there and what they were doing. Carver remembered when he was little. Playing in the schoolyard, he'd see a big plane overhead and wonder where it was going.

That had always been Carver's lot. When he traveled, he wanted to stay put. When he stayed in one place, he dreamed of anywhere else. Sometimes, when he was by himself, he dreamed of finding his mother. When he thought he'd found her, he needed to be alone.

Chapter Forty-one

TUESDAY MORNING

A photograph comprises light and shadow. Sometimes the substance of the picture lurks in those darker areas. To bring it to the surface, you must shade that area of the light-sensitive photographic paper from the enlarger's beam. The process is called dodging shadows. Sometimes Will Carver felt he'd spent half his life at it.

You'd never get one to admit it, but most press photographers don't like that end of the camera, the darkroom end. They get paid to take pictures, and you can't take any if you're up to your elbows in contact sheets and negatives in a small, dusky room.

Part of it is psychological. Pulling a first-rate print usually amounts to corrective surgery. If you shoot news, you rarely have any control over the conditions. The background or lighting might be wrong, or you've got the wrong lens or the wrong-speed film. Or you're fumbling to set the right exposure and snap the picture in the same instant.

Whatever the negative lacks, you try to add on the photographic paper. Every time you pull a print, you're reminded of the ways you failed when you took the picture.

So you settle for something the newspaper can print, pray you got the right I.D.'s for the people in the picture, and try to get back on the street fast as you can. Whether the shot is good or great, it usually has the life span of a mayfly. The day after it appears, it's dead. If you're a newspaper photographer, you're only as good as your last frame.

Carver was one of the few photographers attached to the *News* who enjoyed the darkroom. He liked fussing with the trays of chemicals, and he still got a rush when an image slowly emerged on the photographic paper as he soaked it in the tray of developer. He puttered in the printing room till three A.M. some nights, falling asleep with the stench of hypo still on his hands.

As far as he was concerned, the camera was his Aladdin's lamp and the darkroom was the genie.

Although he hadn't been on the **News**'s payroll in nearly two decades, Carver still hung out in the photo department often enough to merit his own locker off the desk area and that precious work space in the printing room.

The space he shared was cramped—maybe three feet of orange Formica-topped counter space, an enlarger, a beat-up radio, and a couple of drawers to keep supplies—but it offered a convenient spot to sack out. He had to sleep in a fetal position, with his peacoat for a pillow, but the place was quiet after midnight. The amber safelights gave the room a soft if antiseptic glow, and the rent was cheap.

The room itself was impersonal, like a poorly lit high school biology lab. The chemical smell was slightly more acrid than formaldehyde, and the only dissecting to be done was the chief photographer's postmortems on shots that died in the camera.

In the old days, photographers used to complain about the drudge work in the darkroom, hand-dipping each print from developer to stopper to fixer on a precise schedule. Now that technology had made the old process all but extinct in newspaper darkrooms, press photographers griped about losing artistic control. Nowadays, all you did was expose the photographic paper for the right amount of time and run the sheet through the Ektamatic processor. Moments later, out came the print and you were done—the darkroom equivalent of a microwave oven.

When Carver wasn't on deadline, he preferred to develop prints the old way. He wanted the control it afforded, even if his colleagues ribbed him and asked if he'd apprenticed under Matthew Brady.

Tonight, like so many other nights, the darkroom was his refuge. Fighting the urge to light up his last Robert Burns, Carver plopped down on the floor and leaned against the wall under his countertop. His back would hurt tomorrow, but this had to be home tonight. It felt good to be rid of the flak jacket, to be somewhere safe.

The room was so still that he couldn't fall asleep. He reached up and groped for the radio knob. When the sound came up, he realized some lab assistant had tuned in an all-talk station. A caller was complaining about an epidemic of jaywalking in the borough of Manhattan and demanding to know when the police would crack down.

Carver couldn't believe it: Nobody gets stopped in New York for anything but illegal parking or mass murder, and this guy wanted wayward pedestrians thrown in the slammer. Carver questioned the guy's sanity, then questioned his own—after all, he was listening to the moron.

That was the problem with New York City. As most politicians had learned, if you pushed loud enough and long enough, you eventually succeeded.

That must have been Brud's strategy—to keep pushing until he got the damned film back. Now all the rules had changed. Brud would move quickly now, and Carver knew he'd better be prepared.

As he leaned against the smooth wall of the darkroom, he mapped out the next morning. First, he'd head down to the East Village and try to locate Puma. Then he'd try to locate the guy in the blackmail pictures one last time so he could warn the guy about what was going down. Maybe he'd drop by the Other Self on Jane Street and see if anyone recognized a picture of the poor chump. If not, he'd head over to Acey-Deucey's and see if Tracey had come up with anything.

But the more Carver thought about it, the more he understood that the identity of the blackmail victim was immaterial. To get free of this mess, Carver figured, he had to deal with Brud, and there was no telling what Brud was planning now. Brud would probably try to come after the film one more time, only this time Brud would come at him with both barrels.

Carver sensed it would come suddenly. And soon.

Chapter Forty-two

The smell of machine coffee under his nose awoke Will Carver at ten-thirty A.M. Out of reflex, he flailed his arms. Hot coffee splattered onto his shirt. His eyes popped open, but he was too groggy to see in the darkroom's low light.

"Good morning, buddy. Don't be so hostile." The voice had to be Ralph Dempsey's. Everybody else at the *News* knew better than to bother Carver before noon. Ralph flicked on the lights, and Carver's face smarted when he squinted to see who dared to disturb him.

"Yo, bub. Nice way to treat your star photographer."

Ralph stood over him, ten-cent grin on his face. "Thought I'd find you here. I've got a package for you, and I thought it'd be more important than beauty sleep. Although judging from that face, you need all the beauty sleep you can get."

Carver tried to stand, and used the countertop for support when his back stiffened. He hobbled to the sink, turned a spigot, and splashed cold water on his face. His left ear burned.

If Carver at that moment felt a notch above bumhood, Ralph didn't help: "You know, you used to be a hell of a lot sharper on half the sleep. Remember that time you had worked two shifts in a row, were ready to collapse, and you got that tip about the mob dumping a stiff on Delancey Street at four A.M.? And you were afraid you'd sleep through the alarm?"

Carver grunted yes. He couldn't stand peppy people so early in the morning, especially ones who reminded him of things he'd sooner forget: To make sure he awoke in time to take that picture, he had downed four cups of water and used his bladder for an alarm clock. He woke up in time, all right, but had to stop twice on the way to Delancey Street to relieve himself. And the dead body never showed.

Ralph prattled on. "Remember the next day? Everybody kidded that you got stiffed by a stiff. You know, at the rate you're going, you're going to end up a stiff yourself. What the hell happened, you get mugged last night?"

"None of your business," Carver said, and dried his hands on his graying Levis.

"It didn't have anything to do with that killing in Washington Square last night, did it?"

"What killing?" Carter said, feigning a yawn.

"Carver, you'd never cut it as an actor. The guy who got killed was the one you phoned about Saturday night—the guy that nearly got strangled with wire in the East Village. Last night the same guy got blown away by two guys—big fat guy and a white guy in a baseball cap."

"So what?"

"I don't know about Refrigerator Perry, but I do know about you. So when I heard about it on the radio this morning, I put two and two together, and I figure maybe you're doing your shooting without a camera anymore. I figure the cops can figure all this out, too."

Carver grunted. "Ralph, believe me, I haven't killed anybody, and I don't think anybody can identify me as one of the killers. The cops can suspect things all they want, but they don't have any proof."

"I think that's what we journalists call a nondenial denial. Come clean. I can help."

"Thanks, but I'll do just fine on my own. Meanwhile, you said something about a package?"

Ralph flipped a kraft-paper-wrapped box onto the counter and headed for the lightsafe revolving door. "Don't worry. I already checked. It's not ticking. Talk to me when you feel more civilized."

After Ralph disappeared through the door, Carver inspected the parcel, which was the size of a shoe box and neatly wrapped with butcher's string. It weighed about two pounds. It had no return address. The front was marked "Carver the photographer, *DAILY NEWS.*"

Carver tugged the twine until it was free, then ripped off the wrapping paper. Inside the box, nestled in red tissue paper, was one exceedingly large black high-topped sneaker. The tongue had been ripped out, and in its place hung a tag with a note. The words were printed in large block letters:

MEET ME AT SIX BY SHERIDAN SQUARE.
BRING THE REAL NEGS AND A SET OF
PRINTS OR YOUR FAT PAL IS DOGMEAT.

Chapter Forty-three

A package also greeted Brud Siracusa on Tuesday morning. He had arisen early after a fitful night. He had been too pumped up after his showdown with Puma Jefferson to sleep properly, and then he had become too nervous about not getting enough sleep to nod off at all.

He was midway through his daily rowing machine routine when the intercom sounded. He turned down the volume on a game show called "Family Feud" and pressed the button. The doorman came on the line: Someone had left a large envelope addressed to Brud Siracusa, and could he come down and get it?

Brud threw on his gray sweatsuit and loafers and took the elevator to the first floor. In the lobby, he was struck with two things— the sweet pungency of roach spray and the gall of the doorman, who put out his hand for a gratuity as he gave Brud the caramel brown magazine-size envelope. As he watched the bank of numbered lights that chronicled the elevators' whereabouts, Brud had to laugh—he wouldn't have given the jerk money even if he'd had any to spare.

On the return trip on the elevator, Brud inspected the parcel. It appeared to be a letter with a lump in it. He ripped open the envelope as the elevator reached his floor and nearly tripped over a leash connecting a dumpy-looking beagle to a dumpy-looking dowager in housecoat and curlers. She clucked at him to watch where he was going, and the dog snapped at his ankles. The elevator doors closed behind them before Brud could decide which bitch to strangle first. Didn't the old bag know that some people were allergic to dogs?

He checked the narrow hall to make sure it was empty, then extracted the letter. It had been written on an electric typewriter, and it came with a .45-caliber bullet Scotch-taped to the bottom. He saw that the bullet's casing had been engraved with two words: "Brud Siracusa."

He raced through the note, then studied it to make sure he had understood it right. The memorandum was marked "From the Accounts Receivable Dept.," and it reminded him that his debt was "perilously" in arrears. It warned that the debt had now reached twelve thousand dollars because of interest charges that had been compounded daily. It went on to say that if the amount weren't paid in full by the end of the current working day, his account would be turned over to a collection agency.

The last sentence of the note said that the collection agency had a bullet with Brud's name on it. The letter was unsigned, but Brud knew who its author was. His loan shark was never one for subtleties.

Chapter Forty-four

Mornings in late November, the sun casts a fragile light on Manhattan. Even on the clearest day, the sky is tombstone gray and the smell of car exhausts hangs so thick you'd think you were in the Lincoln Tunnel.

Along the Bowery, bums plant their reddened knuckles under their armpits to stave off the chill. Kids who usually play hookey seek the shelter of a classroom. Working stiffs tuck their chins to blunt the wind whipping down the man-made canyons to the north and wish they could afford a cab.

Will Carver usually reserved mornings such as this for sleep or darkroom work, but on this Tuesday, he found himself walking south, the wind at his back, a cupful of deli coffee in his gullet, and foreboding in his chest.

He seldom got that feeling, but when it came he couldn't shake it: a sense of powerlessness, as if a child were drowning beyond his grasp. The last time he'd felt that way a crucial deadline was upon him and the film in his camera was still blank.

In seven hours would be his showdown with Brud, and he sensed, win or lose, that this part of his life was ending. He no longer feared tonight's outcome. One way or another, he would be done with the dirty photos, done with Brud, done with taking pictures for a living.

Earlier that morning, after Carver opened the box and found the high-topped sneaker, he had called Puma's apartment. Puma's mother said her son hadn't been home all night, but unfortunately such behavior wasn't very unusual. Carver gave his number at the *News* to her and told her to call if Puma appeared, but he wasn't holding his breath. Although Carver still planned to meet Brud tonight, he knew that Puma had to be dead already: How do you kidnap a three-hundred-pound teenager?

During the thirty-block walk from the The News Building, Carver toyed with stopping by Gina's and shredding the prints, then skipping town. Too late. In this card game, not only was he low on chips, he had to play out the hand that Brud had dealt him. He had to see it through, learn who held the aces and who held the queens.

Whenever Carver had to shake a brown study, he went through the same ritual, like a warrior psyching himself for battle. So, at Thirteenth Street and the Bowery, he entered an army-navy store and picked out a green flannel shirt and prewashed Levis. He then asked to see the best throwing knife in the place. From a thick glass case the clerk fetched a knife with a retractable six-inch blade. The clerk handed it over, leather grip first.

Carver flipped the knife gently in his hand, and the heft felt right. To make sure, he turned toward a dressing room door five yards away and flicked his wrist. The clerk flinched, and the blade embedded itself in the door. When Carver went to pry it loose, he saw other gouges. He hadn't been the first to test-drive a new knife.

The clerk rang up the purchases hurriedly, then Carver took his parcel and walked east for a block and a half.

Although he went there but twice a year, Carver claimed the barbershop on Second Avenue as his own. He knew Horace would grouse at the prospect of cutting hair that had been pruned over a bathroom sink for the better part of a year, but Carver appreciated the abuse. It was Manhattan's charm—taking grief from a tradesman who acted like he did you a favor when he was only doing his job.

A bell jangled as Carver entered, and he hadn't stepped one foot inside before Horace was shouting to close the door.

Carver took his time.

Horace sat in the second barber chair. He was quite thin, with a drawn face, slicked-back gray hair, and all the charm of a guy who sells car transmissions for a living. He was reading the *Post*, and he made no move to get up as Carver hung his cap, coat, and flak jacket on a hook over the magazine rack.

"Hey, Horace. How's Mr. Congeniality?"

Horace kept reading. "Well, if it isn't Cameraman Carver."

"I didn't know if you'd still recognize me, Horace." Carver pronounced the name "whore ass," just to irk him. "Haven't seen you in ages."

"You don't have to tell me that," Horace replied. "I can tell by your hair. You still butcher it yourself, or you got a blind friend?"

"Spare me the lecture, and give me the usual, okay? Some time today if you're not too busy reading today's beauty tip in the *Post*."

Carver's spirits were lifting. Nothing beats an insult to take your mind off your troubles.

"How often you come here, camera boy, maybe once a year? And you want the usual? What in hell is the usual?" Horace said, and slowly got off his duff.

"You know—long enough to brush, too short to comb."

Horace went into his spiel, although he knew it was futile: "Invest a few dollars more, my friend, and I could give you a continental cut. Look real spiffy for the ladies. And considering how your face looks, you need all the help I can give you."

"Do me a favor. Cut my hair and put a lid on the comments."

Carver sat in the chair nearest the door, and Horace draped a pin-striped sheet over Carver's shoulders. Horace reached for a spray bottle of water and wetted Carver's hair, then tried to comb it straight.

The hair around Carver's ears insisted on sticking out like a matched pair of ski jumps, and no amount of combing would make it lie flat. Horace gave up and took a pair of electric shears in hand.

Over the drone of the clippers, Carver could barely catch Horace's words: "Saw your picture in the paper the day after the pawnbroker got killed. I forgot you still took pictures for the *News*. You must be rich."

Carver started to turn to reply, but Horace twisted Carver's head straight. Carver grimaced when Horace touched his sore ear.

"Sorry, sport," Horace said. "Who beat you up, the dude who killed the pawnbroker?"

Carver said never mind. Horace wouldn't hear of it. "So, you gonna get this place shot up, like the pawnshop? That stuff's bad for business. People won't come around anymore."

Carver turned his head again—resisting Horace's efforts to crank it forward—and replied: "The only thing that's bad for your business is your haircuts."

Horace placed both hands firmly on Carver's scalp and twisted his head back into cutting position. "If I'm such a lousy barber, why come back?"

"Two reasons," Carver said, hiking his voice instead of trying to turn around. "You're the only barber who still charges five bucks. And I got a big showdown this afternoon—maybe with the guy who was behind the killing of the pawnbroker. I want to scare the hell out of him, and what's scarier than one of your haircuts?"

Horace finished trimming and turned to his scissors and comb to apply some shaping. As usual, he got in the last dig: "You know, Carver, you got a lot more gray hairs than last time."

Moments later, Horace undid the sheet, shook off the dead hair, then tied the sheet loosely around Carver's throat. He took a straight razor and scraped the nape of Carver's neck. It burned, but Carver didn't protest.

When Horace reached for the hair spray, however, Carver jerked away. "No way. I came here to have my hair trimmed, not glued."

Horace sighed and tried to comb a part into Carver's hair. After he finished, he held a hand mirror at the back of Carver's head and awaited approval.

Carver didn't disappoint. "Horace, I can say without exaggeration that this is the finest haircut I've gotten in the past six months. You should show the *Post* your clippings."

Carver stood and reached into his wallet for a ten-dollar bill. "Here, and keep the change. I promise not to tell a soul who did this to me."

As Carver donned his flak jacket, peacoat, and cap, Horace shouted: "You really going to see that thug today?"

Carver nodded, and Horace tossed him something. At first, he thought it was a cigar, but when he caught it he realized what it was: the straight razor, folded into its handle.

He tossed it back. "Thanks, but I won't need this. I may have to kill somebody, but I don't plan on skinning him alive."

Chapter Forty-five

A block from Horace's tonsorial parlor, Will Carver removed his Phillies cap and rumpled the part out of his hair. He'd always believed that you couldn't trust a man who fussed with his hair. The philosophy extended to men who used a comb for anything more than ripping out tangles.

Carver checked his watch: just after one P.M. Time was trickling away, and he was getting nervous. Carver knew he never had the patience for details, and now he had placed himself in the middle of a jam where details meant everything. One slipup and he'd be in trouble deep.

Whether he came up with the photos or not, Brud would try to kill him tonight. Carver knew that to survive he'd have to have a plan of his own, and every piece of it had to be nailed tight in the next few hours.

The first step was to go to Joe Gold and see if he could get some reinforcements. He walked into the precinct house at one-fifteen. Gold was expected in fifteen or twenty minutes, so Carver showered and changed into his new clothes.

At one-forty-five, he located Joe Gold in the narcotics room. There, over a cigar and a vending machine cola, Carver made his pitch.

"I need your help, Joe. I know I should have come to you sooner, but I was afraid. Now I don't have a choice."

"You want to run that by me again?"

"I accidentally came across some dirty pictures last week, and the guy they belong to wants 'em back. Says he'll kill me if I don't."

"So give them back."

"I can't. I burned them, Joe." Carver wondered if Gold could see that he was lying. "They were disgusting."

"Disgusting even by your standards?"

Leave it to Gold to joke at a time like this, Carver thought. "And as you can tell from my face, he doesn't believe me. He's meeting me at six-thirty tonight at my apartment. I'm out of options, except for New York's finest."

Joe tugged on his ear and stared out at the lockers to Carver's left. Carver fell silent, and Joe didn't respond. Instead, he unwrapped a stick of gum, folded it in half, and popped it into his mouth.

"Joe, am I boring you? I'm telling you that some creep's going to kill me, and you're thinking about what you'll have for dinner or something."

"I'm listening. Go on."

Carver lost his train of thought. Joe was acting like a damned cop, not a friend—playing it by the book, prodding for more information, offering zero help.

"Forget it, Joe. I thought you'd help me, but you're acting like I'm some geek off the street."

Joe frowned again and rubbed the back of his scalp. "Come off it, Carver. You say you came for help, but you're giving me a line of crap. I wanted to hear your story before reaching any conclusions. Well, now that I've heard it, I have to tell you that I don't believe a word of it. . . .

"I'll tell you what I'm thinking, Carver. I'm thinking that you're holding out on me. I'm thinking about that pawnbroker who got murdered. I'm thinking about the thug tied up in the stolen car with 'I Killed Bingo' scratched on the door. I'm thinking about the same guy being murdered in the Village last night, and an eyewitness saying that one of the suspects wore a baseball cap.

"In short, I'm thinking you're in some incredibly deep crap and you're sinking deeper. I don't know if you've killed anybody, and it doesn't matter because I don't think I could prove it. But we used to be friends, and if you level with me, off the record, I'll do whatever I can. Now, who's behind this?"

"The man's name is Brud. I think he's trying to blackmail

somebody with the pictures. He thinks I have 'em. He wants to kill me if I don't give 'em back. That's all there is to it. You suspect me of whatever you like.''

Joe let out a deep breath and reached for a small spiral notepad. "You really expect me to believe this?"

"Hear me out. Remember when you drove me to my apartment Sunday night, and I said I needed protection? That was why. He finally caught up with me last night and gave me this warning, in case you hadn't noticed.''

Carver pointed to the bruises on his right cheekbone and tried to give a description of his assailant.

Joe scribbled a few words, then tapped the notepad with his pen.

"Well?" Carver asked.

Joe shrugged. "What can I do? I don't see anything I can nail this guy on. It's his word against yours, and like you said, you don't have the pictures anymore. We have a big nothing here."

"All I'm asking is you send somebody over to my place at six-thirty, so I have some protection in case this guy gets violent."

"That's out of the Ninth's jurisdiction, but I'll make a call or two if I can find the time. What if you don't show? Leave town until he cools off.''

"You know me better than that, Joe. I'm a stubborn bastard, and nobody's going to run me out of town. So I'll face this jerk alone. I just thought you could help."

"Something's wrong here, Carver. If you weren't an old buddy, I'd say you're a liar. You don't seem scared. You seem pissed. One last chance to come clean. Like I said, this is all tied to Bingo's killing, your photos, the 'I Killed Bingo' incident, that murder in Washington Square last night, isn't it?"

Carver stood to leave. "You gotta trust me. I'm at the end of my rope, and I don't need you pulling the noose tighter. The guy says he'll shoot to kill me. Just help me by sending somebody to my place at six-thirty. Promise?"

"Like I said, I don't have any jurisdiction there. I'll do what I can, but set me up for some scam of yours or put me in the middle of some horsecrap and your troubles will just be beginning.''

Chapter Forty-six

From the exterior, the Other Self Ltd. was no different from the thousands of other small businesses located in brownstones and office buildings throughout Manhattan: neatly painted logo in the window, professionally printed nameplate by the buzzer, and a sign in three-inch-tall gold letters on the thick white door.

Inside was different—nothing Will Carver could pinpoint immediately, but an atmosphere that kept him on edge. Maybe the carpeting was a little too pale for a place of business, the framed-prints on the whitewashed walls a tad too impressionistic, the country French furniture too fragile.

Carver arrived at the office just past two-thirty, after calling and arranging for an appointment with the president of the Other Self for three P.M. sharp. He got there early in hopes of hanging out in the reception area to see what went on.

To a receptionist named Frances, Carver had introduced himself as a reporter from the *Village Voice* and said he was working on a story about unusual support groups.

Frances sat behind a long, gilt-trimmed white table in the middle of what once had been someone's apartment. Carver had seen her kind before. Quite angular and thick-waisted, about five-foot-seven and one-hundred-fifty pounds, inch-long fingernails painted blood red. Her lavender knit shirtwaist dress stretched across her broad shoulders. Her sandy blond hair said wig.

Frances's voice was a gravelly whisper, and she presented her little sales speech as if she had memorized it: "Welcome to the Other Self. We're a nonprofit group dedicated to helping transvestites deal with their innate desires, to tell them that it's healthier to dress like women than to repress their emotions.

"We provide a monthly newsletter, a place to meet, an encounter group that meets every other week, guest speakers, weekly dinners, social hours every Friday, mail-order discounts. . . . We also network with several other transvestite organizations across America. Did I forget anything? Oh, yes. Membership is two hundred dollars a year. Here is our brochure. Any questions?"

"Are all transvestites homosexuals?"

"You write about us and don't know? Just because we like to dress up doesn't mean we like other men. In fact, eighty percent of our members have families. Those flaming drag queens you see in Times Square give us all a bad name. . . . Now if you'll take a seat on the davenport, Amanda Cooplish will be with you shortly."

Carver leafed through the brochure and tried to eavesdrop on Frances's phone calls, which arrived at the rate of about one every few minutes. Judging from Frances's comments, most of the callers were asking when the next backgammon night was and what dish from Balducci's they could bring.

Carver waited for a lull in the calls, then walked over to Frances. "This brochure and your little speech have been really helpful. In fact, I don't even know if I need to talk with Miss Cooplish anymore. But I do have a favor to ask. The transvestite who suggested I write a story about your group—I took a bunch of photos of him, and she forgot to give me her name or address. . . . Well, I'd like to make sure he gets the pictures. A couple of them are quite flattering. Here's one of the pictures. Recognize him?"

Frances studied the wallet-size photo for a minute, checked the back for writing, then returned it to Carver. "He's certainly not a member here, or I'd know him. The way he dresses and puts on his makeup . . . I don't want to sound catty, but I'd say he's still very unsure of herself. Doesn't come out of the closet much. He does look familiar, though. Maybe a guest at one of our soirees."

Carver fiddled with his Phillies cap. "It's very important that I find him. Maybe fifty dollars would help make sure he got a note from me."

"Please, save your money. If you leave a note and the picture, I'll check around discreetly and make sure he gets your message." Frances handed Carver a sheet of lavender notepaper, a matching envelope, and a black felt-tip pen.

As Carver was deciding what to write, the phone rang again.

"If you'll just excuse me one second," Frances said, and reached for her white Princess phone. She cleared her throat before speaking. "Other Self. Frances speaking. How may I help?"

Frances checked her white leatherette appointment book. "Yes, you can rent the room for the whole night tomorrow. I'll put your name down now. You're all set. Bye-bye."

After Frances put the receiver back in its cradle, Carver got her attention again. "One more question for you, Frances, then I'll let you go. The room you were talking about on the phone just now—could I see it? It would be helpful for the article."

She led him down the hall and ushered him through a white door. Carver peered in. One look made his stomach churn. The room was the size of a typical apartment living room, and it came furnished with all the damning details from the photos. The floor-to-ceiling windows, the floral-print sofa, the framed poster of the famous *New Yorker* cover by Steinberg.

The room looked so pleasant, so peaceful, but Carver could only think of the blackmail photos and the look on the transvestite's face. He felt a chill on his neck.

Carver wanted to leave, but first he had to see where the candid cameraman had lurked. He went over to a walk-in closet, about twelve feet from the sofa. It was empty, save for the discarded little orange box with the red Kodak emblem.

He picked up the empty box and handed it to Frances as he left the room. "I found this on the floor. It's not good for your group's image."

Back at the front desk, Carver remembered to write his note, then placed the sheet of paper in the envelope, licked it shut, and handed it to Frances. "Could you give this to the man in the photo I showed you? The sooner the better. And thank you. You've been incredibly helpful."

The note in Frances's hand was right to the point.

Dear Sir:
Someone is trying to blackmail you. This time they're bluffing. Better return to the closet and change immediately. Your slip is showing.

Chapter Forty-seven

In Brud Siracusa's basketball-playing days, he always detested the hours before a big game. The practices and team meetings were over, and it was too late for any preparations aside from putting his gear in order and making sure he'd eaten the right foods—usually a banana, a bagel, and a quart of water to make sure he wouldn't dehydrate in the heat of the fray.

After getting the loan shark's note Tuesday morning, he hadn't much felt like going to the office and reworking the ledger sheets. If he didn't come up with the money by tonight, work wouldn't matter anyway.

He'd called Stanten at the brokerage house around eleven A.M. and was less than heartened by the secretary's response. Mister Stanten had taken the day off. A call to Stanten upstate was only partly reassuring. Stanten answered and chattered nervously about not being able to pull together the money in time.

Brud reminded Stanten that he had no other choice. To do otherwise would end Stanten's career. Stanten pleaded for another twenty-four hours, but Brud held firm. Seven P.M. at Acey's, or the photographs would go into the mail to the chairman of the board. Period. In his best Clint Eastwood voice, Brud explained that he'd addressed the envelope already, and he read the brokerage's address aloud so Stanten would know that Brud wasn't pissing around.

At three P.M., Brud ordered a plate of buttered fettucine at a local bistro—carbo loading, he joked to himself—then returned to his apartment and laid out gear for the evening that lay ahead. First, he slid six hollow-nosed bullets into the chambers of the

.38 and put it in a leather shoulder holster. Then he slid the closed switchblade into the inside pocket of his overcoat.

At four, he went to a dive on Bleecker Street. He ordered an Amstel Light and asked for his change in quarters. He carried his beer to a battered pinball machine near the front door: time to sharpen his reflexes and get a little adrenaline flowing. He placed his overcoat on a chair, took a sip of beer, then set about conquering the machine, an old Gottlieb called "Fast Draw." The paint on the playfield had been worn to bare wood in several spots, and he soon learned that two of the drop targets required a hard dead-on shot to go down.

The vending company had jacked up the back legs of the machine to make the ball move faster (and make high scores tougher to achieve), but Brud soon got into his rhythm and racked up a few respectable scores.

A three-by-five index card taped to the back glass announced the high game to date, and Brud quickly decided that he had a shot at the record—112,000 points—if he cranked up his game a few more notches.

The machine must have sensed what Brud was after. It turned ornery the next game, sending the ball down the middle untouched or scooting it out the side gutters before Brud could gain any momentum. He started to whack the sides of the machine with the fleshy part of his palms, but all of his thumping, cajoling, nudging, and cursing didn't help. He kept whacking the machine harder and harder, but the last ball sailed between his flippers before he reached 50,000 points.

Brud rammed another quarter in the slot and flailed away with the flippers. Bells rang and lights flashed, yet he couldn't nail the proper sequence of targets to build a decent bonus score. The game ended at 75,360 points, and Brud was down to his last quarter.

While Brud paused to drink his beer and regroup, the bartender sauntered over. "Hey, Blondie, cool it on the machine—it ain't built to take your pounding."

Brud slammed his bottle on the table so hard that some beer splashed out. He turned and stood toe-to-toe with the bartender.

The Last Frame

"It's my quarter, dirtbag. I'll play as I please. And don't ever call me Blondie again unless you want to swallow your teeth."

The barkeep saw the fire in Brud's eyes, mumbled something about taking it easy, and returned to his station behind the bar. Brud wiped his sweating palms on a cocktail napkin, then looked over at the bartender and defiantly pointed his left index finger at him. The bartender shook his head as if to say "Jerk" and turned away.

Brud rolled the last quarter into the slot. He had come here to sharpen his reflexes, and the time had come to get to work. Pinball is an unpredictable game, but Brud had begun to understand the machine's idiosyncrasies. With a combination of deft flipper work, body English, and well-timed whacks, he methodically racked up his score. After he had played three of the five balls, his score was over 95,000.

Brud hesitated to see if the bartender was watching this display of pinball brilliance, but the fool was busy quarreling with a wino at the far end of the bar.

Ball four was a pinball player's nightmare—a rogue ball that rumbled down the playfield, bounced off a bumper, and hopped out one of the side gutters before Brud had a chance to flip. Brud smacked the machine so hard that an empty bottle atop the back glass smashed to the floor.

The bartender looked up from his argument and yelled, "I told you to take it easy over there."

"Check out the score before you go flapping your lips," Brud called back. "I'm about to set the record." Then he pulled the plunger and put the final ball into play. One by one, he picked off the drop targets until only one—the most stubborn—remained. If he connected, he'd rack up enough bonus points to put him over the top.

The ball rolled down to Brud's left flipper, and he cradled it there as he set up the winning shot. He released the flipper button and the ball slowly rolled down the flipper until it was perfectly lined up with the target, then—*wham*—Brud sent it flying. The heavy steel ball met the target flush, but the target didn't budge. The ball carommed to the side, and Brud punched the side of the machine to keep the ball from exiting out the side.

With that, the flippers went dead. The machine had shut itself off. Brud glared at the red Tilt light, then saw his score. 109,990. Enraged, he smashed his fist against the glass atop the playfield and sent it shattering into a dozen shards.

When Brud saw that his hand wasn't bleeding, he rammed the machine into the wall, grabbed his overcoat, and stormed through the door.

A hundred feet down the sidewalk, the bartender caught up to him. He tapped Brud hard on the shoulder and demanded that he pay for the damage.

Brud reached inside his coat, flicked open the switchblade, and waved it in the bartender's face. "Will this cover it?"

The bartender retreated.

During Brud's three-block walk to his apartment, he noticed a newfound bounce in his step. He'd come within a blink of beating the stupid machine. By comparison, getting the better of a scumball like Carver would be a mere bagatelle.

His encounters with Carver had been very much like a pinball game—to score big, he had to keep nudging, adjusting the level of his game as he went along. The farther they got into this little game, the higher the stakes grew. It all boiled down to the last ball, that one unexpected shot that would put him over the top. He had pushed Carver twice and come damn close to tilting, but now he was about to turn the game around. And he had the perfect unexpected shot—the element of surprise—in mind.

Brud's only concern was whether Stanten would cough up the cash in time. In the end, it was always a question of time.

Chapter Forty-eight

Will Carver walked into Acey-Deucey's at four-thirty. Tracey, at his usual place behind the bar, flinched when he saw Carver in the doorway but tried his best to act casual as Carver approached the bar.

"Well, if it isn't the Prince of Darkness." Tracey exclaimed, adjusting his purple cravat. "Two visits in one week. I'm honored."

Carver ignored the small talk and took a stool directly across from Tracey. "You get in touch with the guy in the photo that we discussed yesterday?"

"No. And you never came back with my hundred bucks." Tracey's petulance sounded forced.

Carver persisted. "Sorry. I got sidetracked. Why not save us both the trouble and tell me his name and where I can reach him?"

Tracey dried a martini glass with a bar rag. "Sorry, love, but the price went up. It'll cost you five thousand bucks now."

"That's a little expensive for my blood. Especially when I really don't have to find the mascara man anymore. It's over. I got you and your scam all figured out. Don't act like you don't know what I'm referring to. You and Brud and your blackmail scheme. You're in on it. As I was walking over here just now to see if you'd had any luck locating the transvestite in the photo, I finally figured out how Mo found me yesterday. I told you I was headed for Eighth Street. You must have tipped Brud off, and he sent Mo to knock some sense into me. But nobody attacks me with impugnity."

"Go screw yourself."

Carver grabbed Tracey's necktie and gave it a yank. "Better yet, Tracey, why don't you go screw yourself? You've had enough practice. But before I go, I'd like to tell you a little joke."

Beads of sweat were forming on Tracey's forehead, and he perked up when he thought he might be clear. "Sure enough. Get you a drink?"

"Yeah. How about a Manhattan sunrise?"

"Not sure I heard of that one."

"Shot of vodka, jigger of Maalox."

Tracey laughed a little too hard. "Is that the joke?"

"No," Carver said, lighting up a Robert Burns. "Mine's better than that. It's a little long. But I know you've got the time to hear it."

"Be my guest."

"Ever hear the one about the married guy on a business trip? He meets a floozy in the hotel bar and she takes him to her room for some all-night push-ups.

"Next morning in the lobby coffee shop, a stranger sits beside him, pulls out a stash of photos, and says: 'I think I've got some pictures here that will interest you. Here's a shot of you and the bimbo in the bar last night. That'll cost you a hundred bills. This one is you and the bimbo bluejay-naked in the tub. That'll run you a grand. And here's my favorite—a close-up of you jumping her bones on the water bed. That one sells for ten thou. Whadda ya say?'

"The businessman looks at the photos for a few seconds, scratches his head, and says: 'Okay. Here's the deal. For ten bucks, I'd like a nice eight-by-ten of me and her in the tub. I'll give you another ten spot for four wallet-sized of us in the sack. And as for the shot of me and her in the bar, you can shove it up your ass.' "

Tracey laughed, hollow squeaks in the back of his throat. Carver stubbed out the cigar, mostly for effect. He'd scarcely smoked it.

"Get my drift, Tracey?"

"Afraid not," Tracey replied, wiping his brow. "Why don't you clue me in?"

"I'm saying that if you persist in any more blackmail photography, I'll shove the pictures up *your* ass. While they're still in the camera."

Chapter Forty-nine

Back in the thirties, in Weegee's heyday, the legendary crime photographer once was summoned to a police station to take a picture of a burglary suspect. The guy was handcuffed and seated in a chair in the interrogation room, and he hid his face the instant Weegee walked through the door.

"I don't want my picture took," he said, and legally no one could force him. Rather than try to cajole the thug into posing, Weegee placed his camera on a nearby desk, tripped the shutter delay, and said to no one in particular: "I'm going out for a cup of coffee and a pastrami sandwich." As Weegee left the room, the suspect relaxed, and—click—Weegee had his picture.

Will Carver recalled that story as he crossed Sixth Avenue at Bleecker and headed over a block to MacDougal Street. He, too, needed that element of surprise, something to throw Brud Siracusa off guard long enough to get the drop on him.

In the grey flannel dusk, he heard the peal of church bells. Five o'clock. The witching hour approacheth, he thought. He heard footfalls behind him, approaching fast. He wheeled, fists clenched, only to see a jogger in blue sweat gear stride toward him, breath steaming from his mouth. Time to stay in control—if Siracusa planned something for six, he wouldn't be charging after Carver now. After mulling the notion, Carver changed his mind. Brud was desperate, and that meant he was crazy enough to try anything.

In a pizza shop on MacDougal, Carver wolfed down a couple of slices, then went to his apartment. He checked his mailbox,

The Last Frame

which was crammed with his weekly allotment of bills and circulars. He tucked them under his arm as he climbed the stairs. He patted his peacoat for his new knife, then reached in and opened the blade.

At his apartment door, he gripped the knife with his right hand and awkwardly unlocked the door with his left. He pushed it open and entered. Nobody home but the hermit crab.

"Got some chow for you, Port Authority. You must be starved."

He retrieved a pizza crust from the pocket of his new shirt, tore the crust into small pieces, and dropped them into the terrarium. The crab stayed hid.

Carver tapped the glass. "Relax, bub. In a few hours we'll be home free."

Carver went to the camera bin, unlocked it, and then extracted the .22 pistol. It was still loaded, and he spun the cylinder a click so a bullet would be in the firing chamber. He placed the pistol in his peacoat pocket—insurance in case things got rough in Sheridan Square.

That much was easy. The rest required careful planning and a dose of what every press photographer needs: luck.

When Carver had rented the flat fifteen years before, he'd planned to use the kitchen for a darkroom, and he'd spent a hundred bucks to have the place rewired—when he flicked the switch that activated the amber safelight, it killed all the other lights in the place.

He had also purchased heavy black curtains to keep out light from the air shaft. For the first time in three years, he rehung the curtains. He had always considered the curtains and the new wiring a waste of money, since the apartment was usually too warm to develop a print. Although he had used the room as a studio to shoot an occasional set-up shot, which helped to salvage his investment, it was only now that he realized that it had been money well spent. It just might save his hide.

Next Carver took the throwing knife from his pocket and placed it out of sight on top of the safelight. Then he unscrewed the bulb to the safelight and flicked the switch. Total darkness.

All he had to do was find a way to get a burst of light so he could see to throw the knife at his quarry. Then he remembered Weegee's old trick.

Chapter Fifty

At a quarter to six, Will Carver took a window seat in a dim café twenty yards down the block from the rendezvous point by Sheridan Square. He remembered fifteen years before, when the place had been a decent tavern. Pabst on draft, pickled eggs behind the bar, and a bowling machine.

Sometime between then and now, some genius in a La Coste shirt, designer jeans, and boat shoes had ferned the place. A French name adorned the sign above the entrance, and all the prices had tripled to keep guys like Carver away.

As a result, Carver found himself paying three bucks for a bottle of beer, just so he could watch the street. At those prices, he was in no hurry, and he wasn't about to show his face until he saw Brud anyway.

Every minute or so, Carver pinched back the curtain and checked the street corners by Sheridan Square and the small park nearby, but there was no sign of Siracusa. Carver became edgy, and he absentmindedly read the label on the Michelob bottle while he waited.

He kept running through his plan from here on out, each time growing more and more doubtful that he could pull it off. The idea was to lead Brud back to the apartment, act as though he were getting the photos, then hit the safelight switch. Once the room went black, he had to grab the throwing knife, trip the shutter delay on the Speed Graphic, and fling the knife when the flash unit flared. He felt like the guy who invented Reagan's Strategic Defense Initiative.

What if Brud managed to get off a shot? Carver prayed that it would be at his chest and that the bulletproof vest would do its job. What if Brud aimed for the head? It was over. That's what worried Carver the most—some unforeseen hitch in his plans he couldn't adapt to.

Carver hadn't tested the Speed Graphic, with its slightly bulky Polaroid mount, but its shutter delay and flash unit had never failed in all the times he had used it. He was more unsure that he could throw the knife with any semblance of accuracy under those conditions. If he missed, he would be in for a free-for-all against a maniac, and he could only hope that Joe Gold would keep his word and get some cops over to his place in time to save his sorry ass.

He looked out the window again at Sheridan Square and tried to anticipate Siracusa's moves. Carver had little doubt why Siracusa had chosen the square for the rendezvous point. The area was one of the busiest thoroughfares south of Thirty-fourth Street, with Christopher Street, Grove, and West Fourth all converging on Seventh Avenue in a jumble of traffic lights and crosswalks. That meant plenty of places for Brud to lurk.

And now that night had fallen, the area was taking on a decadent air. Male hookers and weirdos of every stripe came out of the closet to mingle with the tourists and young lovers along the West Village sidewalks.

Carver once more considered bailing out, but he knew he had no choice but to confront Brud and settle the score once and for all. At least this way he had a chance. If he tried to dodge Brud, he'd be spending the rest of his days—or hours—wondering when Brud would put a hit out on him. As it was, Mo had damn near killed him the night before. This way, he had a fairly decent idea of where the bullet would be coming from. And at this point, that was all he could ask.

The next time he looked up, he saw Brud appear in the doorway of the cigar store on the other side of Seventh Avenue. He wore his tan topcoat, jeans, and running shoes. It was ten to six.

Carver left fifty cents' tip next to the beer bottle—he didn't want to die a cheapskate—and started to stand. A hand forced him back into his seat.

Carver turned his head to the right and saw the beat-up leather aviator's jacket. It belonged to a voice that said firmly: "Hey, man, don't leave yet. I just got here."

Carver tried to act natural. "I'm sorry. I don't think you understand. My girlfriend's waiting for me."

The man kept pressing his hand on Carver's collarbone as he took a seat next to him. The man was about Carver's age, short sandy hair with flecks of gray, closely chopped mustache. His voice was pleasant but increasingly insistent: "Guys don't go to this bar to meet girls, and I can tell by the bruises on your face that you like the rough stuff. Don't be getting cold feet now."

Carver bristled. "Hey, bub, I never had warm feet to begin with. I came in here for a beer and a place to sit while I waited for a friend. Now I gotta go."

The man let go and started to take off his jacket. "Relax," he said, "I won't bite unless you want me to."

Carver tapped his fingers on the table. "I don't have anything against you, but I have to leave. Excuse me."

When Carver felt a hand on his knee, he stood, opened his wallet to display Gina's husband's badge, and said the magic words: "Police undercover. Against the wall."

By the time the man obeyed, Carver was out the door.

Chapter Fifty-one

Will Carver raced down the block and dodged the southbound traffic on Seventh Avenue to reach the spot where he'd last seen Brud Siracusa, but Siracusa had disappeared. Carver checked inside the cigar store, then stepped outside and did a slow three-sixty, scanning the passersby, the small park on the other side of Seventh Avenue, the cop standing in front of the subway entrance, the newsstand, the queue of people outside a restaurant. No trace of Brud.

Carver leaned against the side of the tobacco shop and checked his watch. It wasn't quite six P.M. Brud must have showed up early to case the area. He'd be back.

Five minutes later, Siracusa still hadn't shown his face again, and Carver was getting a sinking feeling. He was too easy a target out here on the pavement. . . . Carver looked at his watch again. Six o'clock had come and gone. Five more minutes, and he'd call it quits. Although he had broken out in a nervous sweat, his toes were going numb from standing on the cold concrete.

As Carver breathed into his hands to warm them, a heavyset man in his early fifties approached. He had a three-piece suit, wire-rim glasses, a receding hairline, and a Kirk Douglas chin. His upper lip didn't move when he spoke. "Can I buy you a drink?"

Carver nodded his head no. "Sorry. I'm expecting a friend."

"I've got a nice place and cold champagne."

"I'm sure you do. Now get lost."

The man got huffy. "Look, Jack, if you're not looking for action, don't stand here."

As the man walked away, Carver noticed that the cop by the subway entrance was watching. Great, Carver thought. The last thing I need now is to get arrested for soliciting homosexuals.

Carver turned to leave and bumped into a blonde in a camel hair coat. "Excuse me," he said, but when he tried to step past her, she grabbed his sleeve.

"Got a light?" she asked, and held out a thin brown cigarette.

Carver was reaching for his hip pocket when it occurred to him that the woman must be trying to pick him up, just like that black businessman.

It then occurred to him that since the woman was trying to pick him up near Sheridan Square, then she was probably a he. It also occurred to him that since she wore a camel hair coat and smoked a brown cigarette, that his time was up. Brud Siracusa had finally come to call.

Carver reached for his pistol, but the voice whispered, "Don't bother. In case you're wondering, Carver, I'm not glad to see you. This really is a gun in my pocket. Now let's walk across Seventh Avenue like a pair of old lovers, before we draw too much attention to ourselves."

Carver shook his head and murmured to himself, "It's just like three-card monte."

Brud guided him toward the curb. "What did you say?"

"I said I should have known. It's just like three-card monte. You always get sucked in by the bent queen."

"You lost me."

"I'm just trying to figure out what's the gig with the makeup and wig."

"Simple. Not to think negatively or anything, but if you don't have the pictures this time, I may have to kill you, and I don't want to be seen in public with you beforehand."

The pair crossed the avenue arm in arm, and Brud Siracusa began the negotiations. "Let's skip the chitchat and get down to business. You give me my pictures and I tell you where your fat pal is. I'm tired of dicking around."

The two stepped onto the sidewalk on the other side of Seventh Avenue and walked east, alongside the subway entrance. Carver smiled at the policeman as they walked by, but the cop was looking at something down the block.

Once they were well past the cop on Fourth Street, Carver turned to Brud and continued their conversation. "How do I know Puma's alive?"

"Trust me."

"How do I know you won't kill me the moment I hand over the pictures?"

"That's your problem. If you want to get technical, I could kill you now."

Carver stopped short. "Look, Siracusa. Let's stop the crap. I'm sick of stupid threats, I'm sick of getting my place ransacked, sick of getting beaten up, sick of dealing with two-bit hotheads like you. So you get Puma, the three of us get the negatives, and I never see you again."

Brud nodded. "It's a deal. Let's go. Your fat boy's tied up in the van over there." Brud pointed to a yellow Ryder rental van three cars away.

As Carver started toward the van, Brud shoved him into a deserted doorway and frisked him.

Brud found the .22 immediately. He was looking for a trash can when he saw a cop walking down the block. Sensing trouble, Brud rammed the gun under Carver's rib cage, then kissed him full on the lips. The cop walked by.

Carver tried to squirm free, but the gun barrel dissuaded him. Brud spoke through clenched teeth. "Stay like this for a minute, or I'll have to shoot you."

Out of the corner of his eye, Brud watched the cop walk down the street and around the corner onto a side street.

"Now," Brud said as he stepped back, "show me where you hid the photos."

"What about Puma?"

"Let's just say he won't be stealing cameras or shooting people anymore."

Carver acted confused. "What?"

"It's no big deal when a black kid dies in Alphabet City. It's life. You didn't think I'd let him live, did you? You must have a short memory. The fat pig killed Mo last night, remember? Now tell me where the photos are or you'll join him."

Carver raised his hands above his head. "Okay. I give up. The photos are at my place."

Brud grabbed Carver's lapel. "Man, if they were at your place, I wouldn't be talking to you. I've been through that dump enough times to owe rent."

"Did you look under the lid of the toilet tank?"

No reply.

"I suspected you hadn't," Carver said. "Trust me."

The walk to Will Carver's apartment house took five minutes, though Carver wasn't in a hurry. His instincts told him that things were moving too rapidly, that his plan was going to go belly up, and that he should have brought the photos to the apartment in case it did.

When the two men reached Carver's building, Carver unlocked the front entrance and motioned for Siracusa to lead the way. Brud pushed him inside and presented him with the business end of the revolver. He deposited Carver's .22 pistol in an open trash can in the foyer. "Now move it. And no more crap."

Carver ignored the remark, trudged up the steps, and unlocked his door. The radio was playing an old Tammy Wynette tune. Carver shut it off. Brud removed his wig and placed it in his coat pocket, then wiped off the lipstick with the back of his hand. "Well, where are they?" he demanded.

"The photos? Like I said, they're taped to the toilet lid. I'll get them."

Carver started toward the toilet. The cord to the safelight was almost in reach, but Siracusa grabbed his shoulder. "Hold it. You could have a gun stashed in there. I'll get the pictures myself."

Brud pointed his .38 at Carver and backstepped to the toilet. As Brud lifted the lid to the toilet tank, Carver grabbed the chain to the safelight.

Brud caught the sudden movement out of the corner of his eye, spun, and fired. The bullet hit Carver on the left side of his chest as he grasped the chain to the light, and the impact knocked him backward into the front door. The room went black.

The gun sounded again, and a cabinet splintered by Carver's head.

Carver slumped closer to the floor as he tried to catch his breath. He'd never gotten a chance to reach for his throwing knife. He sensed Brud inching toward him in the darkness. In desperation, Carver fumbled for the Speed Graphic and tripped the shutter delay.

Chapter Fifty-two

Someone once told Will Carver that the only thing that mattered in life was timing. Now, as he lay in the total blackness of his kitchen, he realized that the next few seconds would determine whether he'd survive. As far as he could guess, he had three seconds to slide clear and plan his counterattack before the flash unit kicked in.

He climbed into a crouching position, gasped for breath as silently as he could, and waited. What was taking so long? He trusted the old camera, but now he wished he'd tested the shutter delay. He heard shouting on the stairs outside, but it was probably too late. Brud must be closing in.

Carver trembled. Finally, the flash flared. Brud's gun discharged with a pulse of flame, and the room went pitch-black again. Like a linebacker on a blitz, Carver dived headlong toward where the gun had been. He collided with a kneeling body, and the two men went sprawling across the floor. Carver heard the gun clatter along the linoleum, and he knew he had to find the gun before Brud found him again in the darkness.

Carver scrambled across the floor until he felt the butt of the .38 jam against his ribs. He slid onto his back and grabbed for the handle. While he groped to get his finger on the trigger, Brud was on him, and out of reflex Carver raised his left forearm to fend off punches he couldn't see.

Instead, Carver felt a burning sensation across his left hand, and he pushed with his legs for all he was worth. Brud toppled and Carver opened fire in that direction. Three shots scattered into the darkness.

Brud screamed.

The front door smashed open, flooding the room with yellow light.

Carver swung the revolver around to fire, but instinct stopped him. It was a cop.

Chapter Fifty-three

Will Carver knew it was nothing short of a miracle. For the first time since a stripper had tried to jump from the Chrysler Building back in 'sixty-seven, the New York Police Department arrived in the nick of time.

His first reaction was relief. He was alive, the cavalry had come to the rescue, and Brud Siracusa was ten breaths from the coroner's scalpel.

But before Carver could tell the cops how glad he was to see them, Brud started to plead: "Help me. He shot me. Shot me."

Brud was on his knees, clutching his chest. His hands and white shirt glistened red. His blonde wig hung from the pocket of his open topcoat.

"You—put down the gun," one cop barked at Carver, and he did, nice and easy. He even obeyed when the cop told him to lean against the wall, hands away from his body. One cop frisked him while the other raced out the door—probably to radio for a meat wagon to haul Brud away.

Carver tried to explain what had happened, but the cop told him to save it for the station house. Carver invoked Joe Gold's name, but the cop said he'd never heard of him.

"Then why are you here?" Carver demanded.

"I followed you from Sheridan Square."

"What?"

"I said I followed you from Sheridan Square. You don't remember me? I watched you pick up your blonde drag queen pal over there, and I thought I should see what you were up to."

Carver stood there incredulous.

The cop wasn't buying. "The word on the street is that somebody's been shaking down transvestites. You seemed like a possible candidate, standing on the corner like that, turning down normal homosexuals and then putting the moves on the blonde. So I followed you here, and sure enough, I heard you shoot at Blondie here."

"You don't understand—"

The cop poked Carver in the ribs with his nightstick. "Hey, Mac. Do me a favor. Shut the hell up. I've had my fill of creeps tonight."

The next sounds that Will Carver heard were the whine of sirens on the street below and the click of handcuffs. Only then did he realize his left hand was bleeding.

As the police frisked him, Carver looked down, saw the switchblade on the floor, and cringed. It had never occurred to him that Brud might be concealing a blade somewhere, too. A sloppy mistake, and it had nearly cost him his life.

"Look—the knife," Carver implored. "He was trying to kill me. I acted in self-defense."

The cop scoffed. "Give me a break. Save the crap for the homicide detectives." Then he read Carver his rights.

They had carted Brud out on a stretcher moments before, and Carver heard the fading scream of the ambulance above the rumble of trucks on Sixth Avenue.

Carver felt nauseated. He looked at his hand to assess the damage. It had stopped bleeding, at least—no major veins had been sliced open. He asked the cop for a Band-Aid, and the cop gave him a dirty look.

Carver ran through his options. No matter what happened, the best he could hope for was getting off with some sort of manslaughter rap. The cops would be pushing for Murder One. With any luck, maybe Brud would be DOA, and Carver might have a chance of fast-talking his way out of this mess.

A few minutes later, a homicide detective arrived and got straight down to business. He introduced himself as Detective

Albert Rodriguez and told Carver to sit on a kitchen chair. Rodriguez held a Styrofoam container of coffee in his hand, and he put it on the table as he took a seat across from Carver.

Rodriguez looked to be in his late forties, with a rumpled white polyester shirt and wrinkled gray slacks that indicated he was nearing the end of his shift. His brown eyes were bloodshot, and he needed a shave.

"The patrolman read you your rights? You want an attorney?"

Carver went on instincts. "I don't need an attorney. This is all one big misunderstanding."

Rodriguez suppressed a smile, but his eyes said he'd heard that line a few times in his career. "Okay, Mr. Carver, you've had your opportunity to call counsel. I was supposed to be gone a half hour ago. I want to go home, so let's make this quick. What happened?"

"The guy I shot—Brud Siracusa—attacked me. Plain as that. Look at the bullet hole in my jacket."

Rodriguez stood and inspected Carver's peacoat. "You got another one in your back. You must have gotten it pretty cheap."

"I can show you the welt on my chest."

Rodriguez smirked. "Look, I'm wasting my time here. I think we ought to take you over to the station house, and you can make your statement there. And do yourself a favor. Get a lawyer before you dig yourself in any deeper." Rodriguez motioned for the two patrolmen.

Carver slumped in his chair, then his eyes brightened. "Wait one second. I've got something to show you." Carver stood and walked to the camera as the two patrolmen watched for any false steps.

"Could you steady the camera? My hands are cuffed." One of the patrolmen looked at Rodriguez, then reluctantly obliged.

Carver yanked the sheet of Polaroid film from its magazine and peeled off the back. Rodriguez came over to inspect the photo as the image of Brud Siracusa aiming a gun slowly appeared.

"See," Carver said triumphantly. "He had the gun. I wrestled it away from him. I acted in self-defense."

Rodriguez inspected the photo. "Maybe" was the best he could offer.

But Carver knew he had won. "There's no 'maybes' about it, officer. The camera never lies."

Chapter Fifty-four

WEDNESDAY MORNING

At eight-thirty A.M., Will Carver stopped at a pharmacy on Eighth Street, went to the toiletries counter. He sprayed some sample cologne onto the palm of his right hand and patted his neck. He bought a copy of the *News*, then he headed for the East Village.

He rang Gina Constantine's buzzer and got no reply, so he leafed through the paper. He saw a short item on Brud Siracusa's death, which said in the usual newspaper language that "the incident was still under investigation but charges against Carver could be filed."

Then a wire story on Page Ten caught his eye:

WALL STREET EXEC COMMITS SUICIDE

The story said that a prominent stockbroker named Stanten had been found dead of a gunshot wound Tuesday evening in the den of his Tuxedo Park estate. Orange County detectives at the scene termed the shooting a suicide, and said that a hand-written note found near the body alluded to intense pressures.

The story went on to say that the man had been in line for the top job in his brokerage house, and had quotes from associates and business analysts to the effect that he had been a terrific guy. End of story.

When Gina got home from her exercise class a half hour later, Carver was still waiting in the entryway. He had his Phillies cap on his head and the flak jacket under his arm. His eyes were red and puffy, as though he'd been crying.

Carver thought she might console him, but she kept her distance. All she could muster was a simple question. "It's over?"

Carver nodded.

"What happened to your face this time?"

"That's an old wound by now. Went the wrong way in a revolving door. Story of my life."

"No, really. I heard a little at the cop shop. . . ."

"Talking about it makes it hurt worse. Let it ride."

She smiled—maternally, he thought—and asked him to come upstairs. He returned the smile and followed. At the top of the stairs, she took out her keys and undid all three locks.

She held out her hand, and for a second he thought she wanted him to hold it, but she was merely motioning him inside. "If I seem anxious, it's because I didn't think I'd see you so soon."

"You heard all the details?"

"Let's just say you were the talk of Precinct Nine."

He took off his jacket as best he could, then took a seat on the sofa. Gina remained standing.

"What happened to your wrist?"

"This? The blackmailer used his knife before I could use mine. Fortunately, I grabbed his gun."

"And you're sure that you're OK?"

"I'll live."

"What happens next?"

"I think it's in the hands of the D.A.—what charges to bring before a grand jury. I killed a man. I called the *Daily News*'s lawyer last night, and he said I'd probably get charged with manslaughter, but seeing as how I'm a first-time offender, et cetera, I'll probably get a slap on the wrist and walk off scot-free. Scot free—that's me."

"Then it is over? Nothing else?"

Carver got out a cigar, then thought better of it. "No, that's all she wrote. I guess Joe Gold'll want to talk to me about Mo

Orsinski, but I didn't pull the trigger. I already told him yesterday afternoon about Siracusa and the photos. You heard about Puma?"

Gina nodded. "They found him behind a dumpster this morning. I'm sorry, but I guess that if you mug enough people, the odds catch up with you."

"I'm sorry, too. It sure was nice having him on my side. He saved my life. And because of him, I'm out of the line of fire now. That's why I'm returning your husband's bulletproof vest to you. And his badge. Both came in handy. I know it was tough for you. Thanks."

"What about the transvestite?"

"I couldn't find him in time." Carver showed her the story in the *News*.

"So all of this was for nothing?"

He thought for a moment but couldn't come up with a decent reply. There wasn't any.

She asked if he wanted some coffee, hiding her discomfort when he said that he did.

As she fussed with the coffeepot, he looked around the room. It felt good to be there, to be near her again. He fiddled with the cigar, resisting the urge to light it, and wondered what lay in store.

When she returned, he sat up on the couch, and she handed him a cup and saucer. "Hope it's the way you like it." Then, changing the subject: "You can't stay long. I have to change and go to my mother's on Long Island."

It was a lie, and she felt bad saying it.

"What's the occasion, if you don't mind my asking?"

"It probably never occurred to you, but tomorrow is Thanksgiving."

She was right. He lived in his own little world, a world without weekends or holidays. "And?"

"And I promised her I'd help her get ready. You know, turkey and all the fixings. It's a lot of work."

"Am I invited?"

The question took her by surprise. "I'm afraid not."

"No problem," he replied, masking his disappointment. "I just stopped by to drop those things off and to get my camera equipment."

"And the blackmail photos."

"I don't want them. I should have burned them the day I developed them. Might have saved a life or two."

Gina played with a strand of hair, not an encouraging sign. "Done with your coffee yet?"

"What's wrong?" he asked. "Everything I say or do, you act cold toward me. Two days ago, I felt close to you. I thought maybe we had something going, but now—"

"That was just the emotion of the moment. Circumstances. I thought you might be killed. Then, after you left on Monday, I got to thinking . . ." She hesitated, trying to find the right words.

"Go on. I need to know."

"I don't know how to put it. It's just that somewhere inside you lurks a decent, vulnerable man. But I don't think I could cut through all the armor you've accumulated over the years. Somewhere along the line, you bought your own act—callous photographer, viewing everything in black and white."

"What am I supposed to say? I've learned to keep my distance purely out of self-preservation. If I lived in my own little shell, it's because I had no choice. There's a saying that the only people who can hurt you are your friends and your family—nobody else can get close enough to know your weaknesses. If I don't let anybody get close, I can't get hurt. It's as simple as that. I make no apologies."

She sighed. "I didn't expect you to. But I've thought about who you are and the pictures you take, and I don't want to go beyond a final handshake."

Carver sensed her uncertainty. "Gina, would you please listen? I came here because I want to see you again. It's time for me to drop that armor and get on with my life."

She decided the conversation was going nowhere. Nothing sank in. She walked to the closet and returned with Carver's camera. "But you're still different from other photographers—and the pictures they take. They take photographs for a living. And you . . ."

"I what?"

She handed him the Canon. "And you shoot to kill."

He dropped the camera. Didn't flinch when it clunked to the floor. "I'm done taking pictures." He sounded more certain than he was.

She started to reply, but he stopped her. "I don't mean to be ornery, but I'm not leaving like this. Give me one more chance."

"What did you have in mind?"

"How about starting fresh? You know, when I came here this morning, I was hoping to collect on that backrub. At this point, I'll settle for a friendly handshake, so long as it doesn't mean a final farewell."

When he reached out, she took his hand in both her palms and clasped it against her left breast. He felt her heart pounding.

"Your hand's ice-cold," she said. With that, she took his Phillies cap from his head. Flung it in the direction of the trash can. Wrapped her arms around him and didn't let go.

After a minute had passed, Carver spoke. "Now I know you're crazy about me," he whispered.

"How's that?"

"You didn't even notice my haircut."

"We've got plenty of time for it to grow back," she said, and pulled him gently on top of her.

He started to unbutton her blouse, and when they realized that his one hand was too heavily bandaged to unhook her bra, she undid it for him.

Carver began to kiss her, pausing only long enough to look up and say, "Know what else I like about you? You're all woman."